NKAF

Other Works as Martin Hill Ortiz

Novels

Dead Man's Trail
A Predatory Mind

Short Story Collections (Editor)

The Best Short Stories in the English Language (Three Volumes)

NEVER
KILL
A
FRIEND

NEVER KILL A FRIEND

MARTIN HILL ORTIZ

Ransom Note Press
Ridgewood, NJ

Requests for permissions to make copies of any part of the work should be e-mailed to editorial@ransomnotepress.com.

Requests for review copies should be e-mailed to marketing@ransomnotepress.com.

10 9 8 7 6 5 4 3 2 1

Ransom Note Press, LLC
143 East Ridgewood Avenue, Box 419
Ridgewood, NJ 07451

Typeset and printed in the United States of America

Library of Congress Cataloging-in-Publication Data

Ortiz, Martin Hill.
 Never kill a friend / by Martin Hill Ortiz.
   pages   cm
 ISBN 978-0-9773787-0-8 (hardcover : alk. paper)
 1. Women detectives—Washington (D.C.)—Fiction. 2. Police—Washington (D.C.)—
Fiction. 3. Suspense fiction. I. Title.
 PS3615.R823N48 2015
 813'.6—dc23
                          2014043053

To A.F. and C.H.

1

THE ROOKIE COP swept his damp palm over his holster, signaling to the dozen onlookers to stand back: Don't you dare cross the crime-scene tape stretched across the entrance to the two-story tenement. His pale skin was pimpled with fear, his eyes danced about, his jaw tensed.

The onlookers regarded him with curiosity or pained impatience. Some sent double-barreled stares.

"I live here," an old black man announced. "My mother needs her meds. I got to take her her meds."

"I don't care," the rookie said, widening his stance. The Third Police District of Washington Metro extended from embassies and gentrified townhouses to stretches of urban decay. Upon entering this gritty neighborhood, the officer had stepped out of his comfort zone. Even the ordinary seemed to jitter with menacing intent. The three-o'clock bands of school kids passed by, some stopping to view the commotion. Across the street a pair of teenagers exited a hardware store, one tweezing a paper sack between two fingers. Some children entered a hole-in-the-wall grocery. A gray Malibu, DC plates, pulled up and double-parked in front of the building.

"You can't park there," the rookie said.

"Yes, I can," a giantess responded as she climbed out of the car, a hefty satchel dangling from her hand. Six-foot-four, broad-shouldered, African-American, she had a linebacker's tilt; she leaned forward as she barreled toward him.

"Stop scratching your holster," she ordered. "Your twitching hand tells the crowd you'd take five minutes to dig out your pistol." She butted his shoulder as she passed.

"Hey!" the officer protested.

"See? You couldn't even draw your gun on someone bowling you down." She raised her badge so he had to look up. "Detective Shelley Krieg. The damage is on the second floor?"

"Um ... yeah. Second floor."

She stiff-armed the building's front door, shoving it open.

"How come she gets to go through?" someone shouted.

Krieg halted, then pivoted. "Because I've got this shiny ticket." She flashed her shield.

The old man called out to her, "My mother needs her meds!"

"Which floor?"

"First."

"Let him pass," Shelley told the rookie. "Why'd you cordon off the whole building?"

"There's blood in the hallway," the cop answered.

"Second floor?"

"Yeah. Yes, ma'am."

"Then move the tape to the front of the stairwell. Is the back entrance secured?"

"Yes, ma'am."

"Good work."

She bounded up the steps two at a time.

AT THE TOP of the stairs, a spindly teenaged kid sat folded up, his face buried in his knobby knees. He wore Plasticuffs cinched tightly around his wrists and ankles. His eyes cried out, his nose emptied of snot, he rocked himself gently back and forth. Shelley sniffed. The carpet smelled of fresh urine. His.

A splash of blood painted the tips of his sneakers. His bloody tracks led to a middle apartment where the door hung open, spilling out the only light along the length of the dim corridor. The condition of the overhead fixtures—cracked ceramic and a Medusa's mop of wires—seemed so decrepit that screwing in a light bulb would likely burn the place down.

A patrolman stood guard over the kid. "Brace yourself. It's all kinds of nasty," he warned as Shelley headed toward the light.

More crime-scene tape adorned the apartment entrance, streamers for a macabre party.

Shelley stopped at the doorway. Setting down her satchel, she took out and snapped on vinyl gloves. Before entering, she paused to survey the crime scene. The apartment was cramped, one main room. A fold-out sofa bed, a dining table with two chairs tucked beneath, a dresser, and a kitchen all crowded one another for floor space. A radiator pinged as it heated as though being tapped by a tack hammer.

"Hey, Shel," Lt. Kris Atchison said. At thirty-five, he was four years her senior but acted a lifetime more weary.

"Hey, Atch."

"Better use the booties. The blood is sprinkly. Kind of all over."

With the way Atch blundered about, he seemed to think the purpose of the disposable covers was to keep his expensive shoes clean, not to preserve evidence. He looked the way Atch always looked: every hair in place, a trim crease to his dress pants. He was the only detective Shelley knew who paid for professional pedicures. She slipped disposable covers over her work shoes.

A toilet flushed. Detective Sal "Click" Morretti popped open the bathroom door, wedging his shirt flap under the waistband of his pants, below his low-slung belly, and zipping his fly. "Lordy, it's Shelley," he said. "This crime scene just got supersized."

Shelley ground her teeth and swallowed some well-chosen curse words. She scanned the room. A half-turned key was inserted in the doorknob lock. Others dangled below it at the end of a beaded key chain. Above the knob were three sturdy slide bolts. On the dining table sat a wide-ruled yellow legal pad. It had been moved: Streaks of blood on the table surface joined in right angles to mark the pad's former position. Rows of blotchy green dots filled three lines on the paper—ink bleed-through, a felt-tip pen. No blood spots marked the page. The pad's top sheet had been torn off.

Thin dotted lines of blood criss-crossed the wooden floor. Some had been mushed by skidding footprints. The sofa bed lay open, the top sheet pulled back into a wad. No blood spray over the foundation sheet. A pair of pruning shears rested blade down in the kitchen sink.

A phone lay alongside its charging cradle. Its red light was on as though a call was in progress. She lifted it up to listen but heard only the buzz of disconnection. She returned the phone to its position.

"When does Crime Scene get here?" Shelley asked.

"When they get here," Click said.

A broad puddle of blood bloomed from the space behind the sleeper sofa. Shelley stepped to the side and craned her neck to get a better view.

The victim lay on his back. A light-skinned black male, maybe twenty-five, thin but muscular. The fingers of his left hand had been pruned off at the knuckle; the thumb remained intact. Three of the fingertips lay nearby. As for where the pinkie was hiding, only God knew. A deep-cut impression of an elastic band ran from the corners of his lips along both cheeks: something to hold down a gag and seal in the screams. But what made the scene nasty—as the patrolman put it—the victim's chest had been split, his ribs chopped through and the right half of his rib cage pried open like a swing gate.

The gash through the muscles was a dirty red, the color of day-old meat. The open chest cavity exposed an ugly jumble of pink and gray. The bits of cartilage were the yellow of nicotine-stained teeth while the clipped ends of bones displayed a pearly gleam, jutting out like a ready-to-spring bear trap.

"It looks like it would take a good deal of strength to do that," Shelley said.

"I don't know," Atch said. "With the pruning shears, I'm guessing you just need to be motivated—or a sick mother-fucker."

"PCP," Click concluded. "A dust freak."

"You think everything is PCP," Shelley said.

"Explains the world we live in." Click pointed to the kitchen nook. "I came across a bag of powder on top the fridge. Left it there for CS."

Shelley knelt to examine the stubs of the victim's fingers. Some were raw red stumps, some had the blood coagulated. The perp had lopped off a finger, then waited to let the bleeding stop. Did another, and then another. That would take time. Minutes? Hours?

Dried blood crusted the palm of the victim's other hand. The fingerprints of his thumb and index fingers appeared painted with violet.

Click planted himself in the center of the room and began glancing about and snuffling. Finally, he said, "Krieg? Why are you here?"

"Tate sent me."

"*Tate?*" Click echoed, bridling at the name. Atch froze. "Why three detectives?"

"The captain must have decided this case was special."

"Special as in 'super-ugly'? Or special as in 'moron Olympics'? 'Cause three detectives make for a three-way fuck-up. And where's Kent?" Her partner.

"Personal time."

Click rolled his eyes. "We don't need him and we don't need you. This one's a slam-dunk. We got the brain-dead perp sitting in the hall."

"Why are you so convinced he did it, Sherlock?" Krieg asked. "No-shit Sherlock" was Morretti's other pet name, awarded for the way he looked constipated whenever forced to think. Morretti's instincts were off as often as they were on.

"Because he confessed."

"He called 911," Atch explained. "He blabbed it all. We got the murder weapon sitting in the sink." The shears. "He cleaned them off afterwards. Shows he considered the consequences. He'll have a tough time claiming he was out-of-his-head high."

"Kid's name is Rafael Hooks," Click read from a wallet. "Nineteen. Old enough for a life jolt." Click flipped the driver's license to show Shelley that its photo matched the suspect in the hall. As he did so, the contents of the wallet spilled to the floor. Click dropped down to scoop up photos, business cards, and a half dozen singles. In the process he smeared the blood splatters with his knees.

"You know what? You're right," Shelley said. "Three's a crowd. You two need to hike down the hall and skin some knuckles on a few doors."

"Umm ... Shel, we were up in rotation," Atch said. "We're the primaries. We caught the call."

"And since then Tate made me the lead."

"Tate gave you the lead? Fuck me," Click said. He mouthed a few choice slurs and gave her the evil eye as he and Atch slouched their way to the door. They ducked under the tape and hit the hallway. As he parted, Click added, "You ought to plant that kid in the box. He'll talk to you. People trust you. You're just like Oprah."

Shelley looked around, shaking her head. Crime Scene was going to throw a fit. The two lumbering detectives had managed to smudge the blood on the floorboards. If other shoeprints existed, they would never be sorted out of the mix. If the perp had tried to dispose of drugs and had left any residue in the toilet bowl, Click had flushed it away.

She decided it was time to listen to the 911 tape and question the kid.

2

13:47 P.M., FRI., OCT. 25

"NINE-ONE-ONE, what's your emergency?"

"He's dead." The voice was adolescent but sluggish, words forced through numb lips.

"Someun cut him up but good. There's blood, like it's everywhere."

"Where are you?"

" ... my place."

"What's the address?"

"Three-two-four Oakdale. Number two-twelve. In Le Droit. I need the police."

"Just a moment, I'm dispatching a car." Muffled squawks as the operator spoke far from the mike. Then, "Are you hurt?"

"He's dead. All cut up."

"Are *you* hurt?"

"I feel sick. Someun killed him. I was sleeping. They killed him."

"Are you in danger?"

"I got my door locked. It's just me here. There's so much blood."

"Don't touch anything. The police will be there soon. Do they need you to open the door to the lobby?"

"Lobby?"

"Your apartment building, does it have an outside lock?"

"Yeah. But it don't work. I keep three bolts on my door. I hear a siren."

"The police will be there soon."

"I've got to get out of here. This is NMS. Like a splatter movie."

"Try to stay calm. Wait for the police. What's your name?"

"Raffi. Rafael. What's *your* name?"

"Nancy. Rafael, don't touch the blood. Don't disturb the body."

"My Pumas, my new Pumas are sitting in the blood."

"Don't move them, wait for the police."

"I've got to get inside some pants. For the police."

"Just stay on the phone with me. They'll be there soon."

"I didn't do it. I didn't kill him, Nancy."

"Okay. You'll need to tell the police what happened."

"Nothing happened. I was only in bed, crashing. I felt pissed, he burned me, but I'd never of hurt him. I loved him. He was my ..." The start of hard, choking sobs.

"Who was he?"

"The sirens stopped. The police are outside. I got to get dressed."

"Rafael? Who was he?"

"He was my brother."

3

SHELLEY GAZED THROUGH the one-way mirror of the observation room into the hotbox. Seated at the interrogation table, his ankles cuffed to a hasp on the floor, Rafael "Raffi" Hooks seemed no more than a pathetic smudge of sweat and grime. He'd changed into a police-issued jumpsuit, corrections-orange, paper-thin, and disposable. His urine-soaked clothes had been seized and bagged as evidence. He'd sat stewing for an hour, filling a boxful of Kleenex with his tears and snot. Blossoms of wadded tissues decorated the tabletop. Others surrounded the plastic wastebasket due to poorly aimed shots.

Shelley knew that the next few minutes held the key to closing the case. She'd been misled. The 911 tape was not a confession. It could be a weapon, though. She could use it as a tool to coax the story out of him. Physical abuse—a no-no. Emotional cruelty, manipulation, lying—all part of the game. He'd been given his Miranda rights and said he understood them. Clearly, he understood nothing—and, as long as Raffi agreed to talk, he was as good as convicted.

Shelley believed the key to a successful interrogation was in the preparation. With the details of the crime locked in her mind, she would first catch Raffi in a petty lie. Even a trifling misstatement could be wedged open to release a gusher of truth.

She reviewed what she had so far. A search for a police record uncovered no priors, but at his age a juvie sheet was likely to have been sealed. The bag of white powder recovered from the top of the refrigerator weighed in at twelve grams. As to what drug it held, that would take the backlogged lab a couple of months to say. The victim, Keshawn Davies, Raffi's half-brother, had four priors for possession with intent, all nickel bags. She pored over grisly photos of the crime scene. The pruning shear blades were free of blood and gristle, probably washed clean, although the sink basin was dry, not even water spots. The pinkie finger remained missing. She listened to the 911 call again.

Her last bit of preparation was mental, zoning in on the pitch-perfect attitude. She needed to appear as sympathetic as a lifelong friend while prying the truth out of him. She told herself either Raffi did it or he was covering for someone he'd let into the apartment.

Her partner, Kent Bellotti, sat beside her crunching his fists. Although five-eleven, he appeared less substantial, hunched over the documents, paper to eyeball as though trying to decipher the fine print. His angular face had jutting cheekbones and a chiseled chin. With his wire-framed glasses, he looked more like a bean counter than a detective.

Shelley liked the guy, but since becoming a single parent he was nearly useless, a clockwatcher. A dutiful dad, he snuck off the job whenever possible for kiddie time. He kept handy an apologetic smile and a long line of excuses for wriggling out of assignments. This left Shelley short-handed and resentful. Although she adored the idea of kids and believed in the institution of family, she needed a cop to cover her backside, not Father of the Year.

He's not prepared. It's all up to me.

Kent glanced at his watch. "We should get started. He's crying mommy, mommy, but soon he's going to be screaming for a lawyer."

Shelley knew Kent was right. If Raffi asked for a lawyer, the interview would be over and their best chance at sealing a conviction gone.

As the pair headed to the observation-room door, it opened. Captain Dominic Tate entered. Fifty, balding, he had the sort of scowling jowly face only a hound dog could love.

"You haven't started?" Tate asked.

"We're on our way," Krieg said.

"I've got some fresh intel."

Shelley grunted. She was ready to pounce on Hooks. A late-breaking bulletin might rattle her mental prep. She preferred to deliver surprises, not receive them.

"Just got this from the Prince George's PD," the captain said. "They had a crime in Maryland with a similar MO earlier in the week."

"Similar? What does that mean?" Kent asked. "Do you have the file? Do you have the detectives on the phone? Because this kid's ripe for the picking and we need to know what we're looking for."

"I just got faxed a one-page report. Ernesto Grey, black male, twenty-eight, had his ribs carved open. They found him off Rhode Island Avenue just over the District line. A few blocks west and it would have been a Metro case. PG kept the particulars under wraps, didn't want the drama from the media squawking about some chest splitter."

"So this kid's some kind of psycho fiend?" Kent asked.

Shelley shook her head. She felt her mental prep unraveling. "When did this other murder happen?"

"Early Tuesday."

"What time?"

"After midnight, early in the A.M. That's all I have for now. They sent over just enough for a handshake and an offer to compare notes. Their detectives want us to hold off on our interview."

"No way," Shelley said. "We're pumped, he's primed. This is ours. We're going in now. We'll improvise. Come on, chief."

"Don't let me stop you," Tate said.

Shelley closed her eyes, shutting out all the world, every sound except the thrumming pulse beating on her temples. Her lids lifted. Her hands were steady. Time to get the job done.

4

"YOU SEEM PRETTY bright," Shelley said to Raffi. She planted her palms flat against the interrogation table. She did that when she had to sell a lie. It steadied her: no flinching, no tics, no tells.

Pretty bright? After offering up a whopper that size, she felt lucky a lynch mob of saints didn't drag her straight off to purgatory.

Pretty bright? With his ankles chained to the floor, he still hadn't figured out that he could simply demand a lawyer and refuse to talk.

Raffi Hooks had proved his doorknob IQ the moment he agreed to speak to the police. His brother butchered in his locked-tight one-room apartment. *But, hey, I slept my way through the hours of torture.*

He sat crumpled up, bony elbows poking the tabletop, chin cupped in his hands, his eyes downcast.

Instead of refusing to talk, he wore "*I didn't do it*" as though it were a suit of armor.

How did it happen?

I didn't do it.

You were there.

I didn't do it.

Then how did it happen?

I don't know.

You must know something.

Maybe somethun—only I don't know. I want to talk to my mother.

Kent leaned, holding up the wall, arms folded. Standing behind Raffi, out of the kid's line of sight, he smirked his way through the answers. From time to time, Raffi glanced over his shoulder, looking to Kent for approval.

"I found him all bloody when I woke up." "I didn't hear anything." "My door's got three good bolts and they was set tight." "Keshawn didn't got my keys." "I didn't let him in." "Nobody got my keys." "Yeah, I own some shears. I do yard work. They's in my closet."

"They were in your sink."

"I didn't put them there."

He convulsed as though sobbing but no tears came—cried out or just play-acting his emotions.

"You're pretty bright," Shelley said again. "Look at it from our perspective."

"Perspective?"

"Look at how we see it," Kent said, making a slow transit to stand in front of the suspect. "You're telling us no one else could have done it. Or maybe ... what I'm thinking is maybe you had a good reason to do what you did."

"I didn't do it. I loved him."

"That's the funny thing," Shelley said. "I listened to your nine-one-one call and you said you were mad at him."

"I wasn't mad."

"You said you felt pissed. He burned you. How was that?"

"It don't matter. I didn't kill him. I never done no crime and no time."

Kent pulled an evidence-bagged pack of powder from his pocket. "Maybe you can explain this dust."

"I don't dust," the kid said.

"We found this on top of your refrigerator," Kent said.

"My doctor gave me that."

Kent chuckled. "Your doctor gave you a bag of white powder?"

"It's Ritalin. I pound out the pills so I can mix them with juice. They go peaceful on my stomach like that."

Shelley flinched. What the kid said made an agonizing sort of sense.

"Maybe you peddle it on the street," Kent said. "Supplying the junkies with a little Vitamin R? Or do you try passing it off as something hardcore?"

"I don't do drugs and I don't fling them. I want to go home now. I want to talk to my mother. Does she know about Keshawn?"

Shelley signaled to her partner, tossing her chin in the direction of the door. He seemed reluctant to move, so she tugged Kent's shirt sleeve, telling Raffi, "We'll go track down when your mother is going to get here."

5

AFTER SHELLEY AND Kent stepped out from interrogation into the detectives' bullpen, Shelley wrung her hands and gave a kick of frustration to a desk leg. "I was all set to go in there and nail him, I really was. Then the captain tosses out this news flash about some other murder. Ritalin doesn't make a person loony. And does this kid look like a serial psycho to you?"

Kent shrugged. He eyeballed the wall clock as though it were his boss. Going on six, Friday night; the interrogation was already cutting into his weekend family time. "Listen, Shel, the kid's guilty. He had the means—the pruning shears, the motive—he was mad, his brother burned him, and the opportunity—he's as much as admitted no one else could have done it. The jury will head into the deliberation box, crack open a couple of cold ones, laugh at his story, and vote guilty. We got that much already *and* he's still talking. We'll pull a confession out of him. We've just got to go back in there and be brutal."

Shelley looked around the detectives' office. The word must have gotten around about the shocking nature of the crime. All eyes were upon them. Morretti sent a subtle sneer her way.

Atch chimed in. "The crime-scene people say they got a clean thumbprint off of the pruning shears' blade."

"A single print?" Shelley asked.

"That's what I heard."

"Raffi's?"

"We'll know that when you book him."

Something about what Atch said didn't sit right with Shelley, but it took her a moment to get a handle on what. *Okay, first of all, of course he'd have fingerprints on his own tools. But why was only one fingerprint found? Why on the blade? And why no blood on his clothes? If he changed, where did he stash his bloody pants and shirt? And ... and ...*

Kent finished texting a message, then looked up to find Shelley standing, arms folded, next to the door to the interrogation room. Opening the door, he gestured for Shelley to enter. "Lady detectives first."

Rafael Hooks sat tall in his chair, glaring at them.

"We talked to your mother and she's on her way over," Kent said. Shelley noticed, not for the first time, how easily lies came to him.

"She don't got a phone," Raffi said.

"We caught her at a neighbor's."

"In the meantime," Shelley said, "let's clear a few things up. You had blood on the soles of your shoes."

"I could hear the cops was coming soon and I had to get on some gear and my Pumas was setting in the blood, still I took 'em. I can't go out with my feet naked and I had to get out and away from there."

"You had to escape before the cops came?"

"No! I hung back, I waited. I unlocked my door for them. Then I tried getting out into the hall, only one of them flashed his burner. Serious, like he was ready to pop me. He shoved me to the wall, then tripped me so I was on the floor, face down. He strung me up tight, my wrists and my feet. It hurt bad. He made me set, squat in the hall, there by the stairs. He wouldn't 'low me getting up nor any kind of moving, slamming my shoulder whenever I tried rising. Even when I was dying to take a piss, he wouldn't even let me up."

"How sad," Kent said. He leaned in close to the suspect, waving his partner back. "So, this is what I can't figure, Raffi. You're telling me your brother had his fingers chopped off. He got his chest cut open. Blood gushing and he's screaming for his life. And all the while you were two feet away dreaming about My Little Ponies until—what? One o'clock in the afternoon? You know, we never found all of his fingers. Tell me, shithead, *what the fuck* happened to the missing finger? Did you flush it down the toilet? Is it stuck in your garbage disposal? Did you eat it?"

"No! Fuck! No!" Raffi looked to Shelley for help.

Kent moved to block Raffi's view of Shelley. "You said you were angry at your brother!"

"I wasn't."

"Liar! You told 911 you were angry at your brother."

"Did the lady tell you that?"

"It's on the tape. Remember, Raffi? We talked about this. We listened to the tape, we heard you in your own words. You were angry at him. 'I felt pissed,' you said. Mad as hell, right?"

"No!"

"If you fuck with us, if you lie to us, we can't help you, Raffi. And you *are* lying!"

Bad cop, good cop, Shelley thought. Not having prepped for the interrogation, Kent had decided to go primal. Nothing to do but play along. She told Kent, "Calm down!" Then, to Raffi, "My partner gets juiced up sometimes. I'm sure you had a good reason to be angry."

Raffi pinched his nose, cleaning off a drip of watery snot. "He stole my drugs," he said. "He was always stealing my drugs."

"Here's a bulletin," Kent pointed out. "You told us you didn't use drugs."

"My Ritalin pills. He made me pound them up so he could sell them like they was street dust. He was always swiping my stash to sell. But I need my meds to keep my head in place."

"So you need the Ritalin?" Shelley asked.

"To keep my head straight. And when I go off cold, it messes with me."

"So he made you come down from Ritalin," Kent said. "That can be cruel. Crashing, maybe going zombie. Blacking out?"

"The zombies? I get the all-overs. The jumps or hot or cold or crashing. He did that to me. He made me crush up my pills and save them for him. Yeah, that got me pissed."

"So your brother showed up to rip off your stash. You let him in."

"No! I didn't let him in! I didn't let no one in that night!"

Shelley said in a soft, calming voice, "He was in your apartment, Raffi. That's where we found him. Your door was locked."

"I didn't kill him."

Kent slammed the heel of his palm on the table. "You saved your pills for your junkie brother and he didn't give a damn that he put you through hell. Your mind was jumping, you were out of control!"

"No!"

"You killed him and then you blacked out!" Kent said, banging the table again, this time with his fist. "You killed your own brother and you don't even remember."

"No!"

"If you blacked out how could you know?"

This idea seemed to confuse Raffi. He massaged his throat, his mouth gaping as wide as a beached trout gulping for air. Finally, he said, "It was me?"

"Nobody else could have done it," Shelley said sweetly.

Rafael proved he was not all cried out. Tears came streaming down his face. "I didn't want to hurt him."

"You didn't want to," Shelley echoed.

"I need you to say that, clearly into the mike, so everyone knows it," Kent said. "I didn't want to kill my brother."

"I didn't mean to kill Keshawn," Rafael said, his voice flat. His shoulders slumped and his arms trembled. He pressed his fist against his lips. "No! How could I of done it? I didn't. I want to talk to my mother, now."

"Soon. Only one more thing," Kent said. "Who is Ernesto Grey?"

Rafael looked puzzled. "Ernie?"

"Who is Ernie?"

"He's my friend."

"When did you last see him?"

"Tuesday night. He was hooking up with AZ."

"*The* AZ?" Shelley asked.

"No. Just AZ," Raffi said.

Kent smiled and asked, "Why'd you kill Ernie?"

"What?" Rafael tried bounding from his chair but his ankle cuffs held him in place. "Ernie's dead? Let me out of here. I want to talk to my mother."

"You're not going anywhere," Kent said. "And your mother isn't coming. We never called her."

Rafael looked at the two detectives as though they had just taken off their masks, revealing the monsters underneath. "I want out of here! I want a lawyer!"

6

By the time Kent and Shelley finished their paperwork the hour neared nine. Shelley felt numb, but not numb enough. The brutal murders, the pathetic kid calling for his mother, the half-assed confession: None of it seemed to fit together. They closed the case only because they slammed a square lid over a round manhole. It didn't seal in the stink.

Shelley hoped the kid would have a miraculous stroke of luck and get some good representation. She tried telling herself it was no longer her problem, her job was done. But she couldn't let it go.

Okay, come Monday, I'll look over the Maryland files, she promised herself. *I'll talk with their detectives and take a peek at what all Crime Scene dug up ... Maybe chat with Raffi's mother. When all the pieces are filled in, it will start making sense. Maybe.*

"I figured we'd run late," Kent said, "so I texted my babysitter and told her I'd be there at midnight. We need to rinse the taste of this case out of our mouths. Pete's?"

Shelley bristled. "Pete's?" A watering hole, hell after hours. She didn't often visit the place, but what Kent said made sense. She needed to decompress. She needed to dive into a beer and drown the day's bitter aftertaste. Her partner's company would make the visit tolerable.

PETE'S ON TWELFTH and Euclid was a police bar run by an ex-cop, a thirty-and-out pensioner who could let go of the badge but not the camaraderie. The alpha dogs who prowled the streets all day escaped to its refuge at night to down beers and hard liquor and trade jokes only they would laugh at. Sometimes they hooked up with police groupies, lovers, or fellow officers—secrets that they all shared but never revealed.

Tate had once warned Shelley, "Five years on the detective beat and no one but a fellow cop will understand you. Not even your family will know the real you, the one you've got to hide. The one who spends all day gobbling up pain and all night trying to shit it out." On nights like these, she knew he spoke the truth.

Although Pete's boasted live music on Friday nights, this Friday the bandstand stood empty. No music at all, just rumbles of chatter punctuated by whooping laughs.

Shelley and Kent sat at the bar. Her height brought stares from the patrons who hadn't seen her before. She'd become used to it. She felt proud of her height, enjoyed being different—although some days she wished she were a different sort of different. At thirty-one she had dated only men shorter than herself. She knew tall ones existed; she'd sometimes passed them on the street. More often she would meet up with men fixated on tall females, "height hounds," kooks who viewed her more as a totem-pole goddess than as a woman.

Kent drank twice as fast as Shelley, who ranted about the case.

"The pruning shears," she said. "They were polished shiny, sitting blade down in an empty sink. Raffi supposedly washed the blood off. But he didn't wash off a fingerprint? Blood, gristle, hair, that's hard to get rid of. Fingerprints, a little water and they go poof."

"Okay. So he washed off the blood and then handled the blade after it dried."

"Or it's not the murder weapon. Why were there no water spots in the sink? Water mixed with blood should have left specks. And who the hell blacks out from Ritalin and changes into a killer?"

"He seemed to think it could happen."

"And AZ? Freaking AZ. How is AZ involved?"

AZ was practically a legend, a drug dealer who renovated crack houses and turned them over to the poor before fleeing to his next hideout. Never booked, never ID'd, he was equal parts Robin Hood and Bigfoot.

"And what happened to the pinkie finger and the bloody clothes ...?"

"Stow it, Shel. You know the difference between you and me? You came here to stay mad. I came here to shake it off. The job can wait until Monday."

Shelley sucked on her beer bottle to stopper her mouth. Finally, she said, "It's been a while since we just chatted. You seeing somebody?"

"Sort of."

"Sort of" was Kent's term for "just sex." "Your 'sort-of' relationships usually don't end well."

"Neither did my marriage. You got someone?"

"Nope."

"Prospects?"

"Nope."

"You got a friendly checking out your six." Kent shook two fingers in the direction of the jukebox.

When Shelley looked over, a man nodded to her, then turned his concentration to choosing music. Ebony, tall, he had a bull's nose—a broad flat ridge and flaring nostrils—and a wisp of a smile. He didn't seem to have the prickliness of a cop, but he did display a policeman's self-confidence.

His music selected, he picked up a pair of drinks and began swaggering toward her.

"Arrogant bastard," Shelley said. As she looked to Kent for sympathy and rescue, she found he had spirited himself away.

The man sidled atop the adjacent stool. His eyeline was an inch below hers, but he had long legs buckled beneath the chair. He set a Manhattan in front of her, her favorite but something she hadn't ordered that night. He must have had an inside source.

He lifted his drink in a toast. "You're the second most beautiful woman I've ever seen."

Shelley grinned and shook her head. She didn't want to play along, but she had to ask. "All right, then, who's the most beautiful?"

"My wife."

Shelley's grin collapsed. "At least you're honest." She took a deep swallow of the drink, set it down, and tapped her nails on the bar.

"I wanted you to know ..."

"Because otherwise it would be ... *cheating?*"

"Um ... that's half the story."

"And the other half?"

"I'm Taylor Jackson Singer." He stuck out his hand. She let it hang there.

"Your parents liked last names."

"And you are?"

"Someone who doesn't date married men. Tell me: How did you plan for that pick-up line to play out?"

"I had a line, a clever response, and a story, but it all kind of got derailed by that look on your face."

Shelley raised her drink in a toast. "It was a fun train wreck while it lasted."

Taylor quietly nursed his drink, not quite making eye contact. When it was empty, he set the glass on the bar with a decisive thump.

"Tell you what. Let's start over." Taylor Jackson Singer tapped his watch crystal. "It's 11:30. You'll be Cinderella, I'll be the prince. Let's dance until midnight and then you can drive your pumpkin home."

Shelley had never, would never, sleep with a married man. She usually refused to flirt with them. But—she needed a half-hour's worth of fairy tale. She downed the remainder of her drink in a gulp, nodded, and followed him onto the empty dance floor.

On most occasions, she felt unenthusiastic and awkward as a dancer. She dreaded the dance floor, having attended too many socials with short boys' heads planted between her boobs. Now, however, the jukebox played a choice bit of shimmying Motown, and the drinks infused her with the buzz of a bee. She wished police regs allowed her to wear dreads. Her tight-cropped hair left nothing to shake.

The tune lasted about a half a minute before switching to a slow song by Boyz II Men. *Desire porn.* He had chosen the music, planning this out. Two steps ahead of her, he was manipulating her reactions.

Shelley had lived enough years on her own that her loneliness acted as both poles on a magnet. Forces inside her wanted both to pull him in and to push him away. She kept him at a measured distance, her arm stiff against his shoulder, safe-dancing the way the nuns insisted back in junior high.

She felt the turbulence of incompatible impulses. Anxiety and hope, desire and defiance.

Run away, Cinderella ... Surrender.

"My wife ..." Taylor began. When Shelley glared, he amended this to, "My ex- I mean. We're ... disentangled. Divorced."

They locked eyes. Shelley used her detective instincts to gauge his sincerity. He was telling the truth about his marriage. At the same time, it seemed he was holding onto something much deeper. *But then who doesn't have secrets?*

He smiled, big and easy.

"Disentangled?" Shelley echoed. She leaned in against him. They were the same height; her chest matched his. It felt right. He fit.

Tangled, disentangled. I'll sort it out later, she told herself. *It's only dancing. Until midnight, I'll be an Amazon Cinderella in size twelve shoes.*

"You're a little woozy," he said.

"Damned right."

"What's your phone number?" he whispered.

How could it hurt? She answered by whispering back, each number dialed around the circle of his ear with a tingling breath. He repeated her number back. For each digit, he nibbled her earlobe that many times. Two-four-three ... she particularly enjoyed nine.

When midnight came, she kissed him, a lingering tongue thrashing. She felt his hand slip into her pantsuit's back pocket. It left behind a card. She patted her butt, happy. If he hadn't left a card, she'd have had to play detective to hunt him down. Or maybe she would have reversed roles, clubbing him on the way out to steal a princely shoe.

"Give me a call," he said.

"We'll talk."

As she drove home the Boyz II Men song buzzed on her lips.

7

SHELLEY TRIED TO hold onto her dream, certain it was telling her something important, but its warning slipped through her grasp like smoke between her fingers.

Her eyes flashed open. Still night. Her watch, an intense bit of architecture with dials inside of dials, lay on its side on her nightstand. Its luminous face read 4:55.

It took Shelley's buzzing mind a moment to become aware of the silence: the refrigerator motor, the ever-juddering heat vent, the purr of her air purifier—all quiet. Absent were the LEDs of her video player and the pinpoint indicator lights of her stereo, charging cradles, and house alarm. The electricity was off. Her SpongeBob clock had tumbled to the floor, stopping at 3:38.

A stir of breeze chilled the room. A tea candle's flame shivered in an earthen jar, the rim projecting a pulsing halo on the ceiling. The air tingled with French vanilla.

With a gasp she realized she hadn't lit any candles.

She bolted up, took to her feet, and was greeted by dizziness. Her mind felt sluggish, the world unreal. It was as if she had woken from one dream directly into another. The fringe of her T-shirt jammies shimmied just below her hips. She looked in the jar that held the candle, gauging the amount of melted wax. She estimated the candle had been burning for an hour. She'd been sleeping for four.

The nightstand drawer—where she kept her firearm—was ajar. She tugged it fully open, grabbing hold of her .22 automatic. It felt light, insubstantial. She shucked and inspected the magazine. Empty. Someone had made the effort to find her weapon—simple enough—then take out the magazine, unload the clip, replace the empty magazine, and return the gun to the drawer. At the same time, she'd been lying in bed, vulnerable, an easy target for a quick bullet.

Each night, before stowing her firearm, she inspected the firing chamber, chucking out a cartridge when she found it loaded. She noticed a single bullet in the drawer, trapped in the space behind her Zondervan Bible. She locked the gun, chambered the bullet, then unlatched the safety.

Her visitor had left open the door to her bedroom. At the end of the hall, the bathroom door also hung open. From that direction came a heavy whispering sound. *Someone on a cell phone?*

She stood frozen for a moment, her firearm raised, held steady between two hands. Her mind felt fogged over, as though all of the world's coffee, adrenaline, and cold showers couldn't slap her to life. She struggled to focus and consider her options.

Call the fucker out for a showdown. *With one bullet?*

Get the hell out of here. Behind the drawn curtains, her bedroom had a bay window with diamond panels held in place by metal grilles. Breaking out would be a struggle and she'd be a sitting duck trying to cross the lawn.

Call for back-up. She only now noticed her phone was missing from its charging cradle. She saw it lying on the floor, near the foot of her bed. As she walked over to retrieve it, she felt a moist smoosh between her toes. Blood. On the far side of her bed, in the wedge of space alongside the wall, a body lay on its back, its ribs chopped through, its chest cracked open. Thirtyish, naked, a skinny black male, his face covered by a pillow.

The inside of her head became a whirlwind of orders, all screaming at her, commanding her to run, fly, hide: Head to the closet or the front door, dive through a window, do all of these simultaneously.

She picked up the phone, discovering it was sticky with blood. Its battery had been removed. *The fucker hoped I'd grab the phone. He wanted me to leave my bloody fingerprints. He wants me to contaminate the whole damned crime scene.*

More whispering from the bathroom.

What *doesn't* he want me to do? What would catch him off guard, surprise the crap out of him? *Rush him, head on.*

The house sat on a slope, so that its rear windows were set at the level of a second floor. She would storm the bathroom. If she found it empty, she'd lock the door behind her and climb out of the window, dropping into the back alley. The alleyway provided plenty of cover. If someone was waiting in the bathroom, she would do battle. Having emptied her gun, the fucker wouldn't know she still had one bullet. He'd probably jump in front of her for an easy shot.

Her sweatpants lay on the floor, rolled down to the cuffs. She woozily stepped into them, tugging them up. The waistband snapped into place. She slipped into her sandals. Her temples thumped: war drums.

Five doorways lined the hall to the bathroom: three on the left, two on the right. These led to the den, the basement, a closet, and two other bedrooms. She rushed down the hall, entered the bathroom in a crouch, and spun a three-sixty with her gun pointed and her finger on the trigger. She stopped, planting herself on one knee. To her side, the wind rustled the bathroom curtains. The window had been smashed out from the inside. Behind her, the door to a towel closet remained closed. In front of her stood the shower stall, its frosted door shut. Through the frosted glass, she could make out the murky image of a large man, black clothes, short sleeves, cream-colored arms, a ski mask hiding his face.

"Get down!" she shouted. "Face down!"

She heard the closet door creak open behind her. Before she could turn, something heavy struck the back of her head.

8

THAT SAME DREAM, the one that tried to warn her. In it she heard whispers from somewhere distant. *Careful!* her cop-voice advised. *Whispering means two people—one across from the other, one talking, one listening. Don't turn your back.*

Shelley woke up, the crown of her head thudding, hammer on anvil. The bathroom floor felt frigid. She shuddered and tried to grasp hold of a breath, but her chest convulsed and she could only choke out tiny coughs.

A soft grayness filled the room. Dawn had arrived through the back window, but the sun had yet to crest the trees. Her finger rested inside her gun's trigger guard. Still on her back, she raised the gun, aiming side to side as she examined her surroundings. The towel closet lay open. So did the shower stall.

Collecting her wits, she grabbed hold of a thought. *They didn't want to kill me. If they did, I'd be dead.*

Shelley rolled over, raising herself onto all fours. She shook herself into full awareness, then climbed to her feet.

Holding her gun at a handshake angle, she tramped through her house room by room, the first floor then the cellar. Daybreak had chased away the horrors that could be lurking in each shadow, and now every corner stood vacant, unremarkable, as though her home had just awakened from an innocent and typical night's sleep. She flipped the master switch on the circuit box. Her house rumbled, then purred with life.

The alarm reset. She punched in the code on the pad in the entryway. The house was clear; the intruders had fled. She was inside and they were out. She entered her kitchen, lowered her gun, and leaned her butt against the table.

How did they get in? How did they disable the alarm?

Remembering the corpse, she returned to her bedroom and carefully lifted the pillow from the victim's face. She recognized him. Cassidy Higgins. They'd been friends in high school, both in the debate club. Since then she had gone on to a career in law enforcement while he'd become a junkie. She'd seen him here and there on the streets, calling on him now and then as a snitch.

She noticed her cell phone's battery resting in his chest cavity on top of a deflated lung. She weighed leaving it there for the crime-scene techs. *Hell, I've mucked this scene up enough already.* She plucked it out, using her nails as pincers.

She snapped the battery into her bloody phone. She considered whom to call. 911?

She could imagine the conversation. *I slept through the murder. I don't know how they got in. I didn't do it*. This whole set-up seemed intent on humiliating her, transforming her into Raffi.

Who would do this? her mind shouted. *What kind of sick ...* No. She had to focus on the matter at hand. Whom to call.

Her partner. She dialed Kent.

"Hey, Shel." His voice sounded sleepy.

A female voice whispered, "Who's that?"

"Nobody," Kent responded.

"Kent, I need you," Shelley said.

"How?"

"I need you here, at my place. I've got a situation."

"Jeez. I just, um ... you know, it's Saturday."

"It's an emergency."

"I've got Kimmy. Can I bring her?"

"Kent, this is serious."

"I'm not like a divorced father with time-sharing rights. Toddy just up and left, gone for good. I can't divide up Kimmy. I'm a twenty-four-hour dad."

She'd heard this argument many a time.

"Never mind," Shelley said. "Have fun. See you Monday."

"Jee ..."

She hung up.

Whom to call? Tate, her supervisor. This whole affair was about to become a circus soon enough. Might as well start the show.

She only now noticed she had one missed message. She dialed into voice mail.

"Hi, Shelley? This is Taylor," the message began. "Just checking in to see if we're good. I wanted to clear up a thing or two ..."

This can wait. She cut the message short. She clutched the phone, screwing up her courage. When she called in the police she would initiate her second home invasion of the day.

The phone rang, startling her.

"Hello?"

"Krieg!" It was Click Morretti. "Kick the girl out of your bed and get your ass to HQ. We've got a shit-geyser here. Your case has blown to hell and we're all covered with ..."

"Yeah, Click, I get it."

"This is serious. Tate says now. I can't get Bellotti on the line." Of course, Kent would have taken one look at caller ID and chosen not to answer.

"I'm on my way." She hung up and pressed the phone against her forehead. She had to think. Imagining the questions buzzing around in her head as a nest of angry hornets, she tweezed them out, one by one.

How did the trespassers get in?

How could I have slept while they killed Cass?

Why Cass?

Why me?

The realization came to her with a chill. This murder mimicked the death of Keshawn Davies. Who knew she was in charge of the case? Raffi, by now a few he had told—*and the police, her fellow officers.*

This murder had a forensic savvy. It was staged to get her hands bloody, to make her part of the story. Who had the smarts to do that? *The police.*

But why go through all this trouble, invading her house, copying the Davies murder? The answer seemed clear. With these murders matching, she would be a witness—and a suspect. She would be neutralized, taken off the Rafael Hooks case.

You sons of bitches. You're not getting away with this.

A plan formed in her mind. She dialed a number.

"Mira?"

9

Yasmira Tamer worked at the Central Forensics Lab. She was the only person Shelley would entrust with so dark a mission.

They first met back when both were rookies. Shelley had been sent to the crime lab, assigned the task of babysitting some urgent evidence and waiting out the results. While Shelley was lunching in the break room and nibbling on pastrami, Yasmira brought over a tray with soup broth and a dozen packets of saltines and took a chair opposite her.

She was rail-skinny with a pixie's face and six piercings trimming the crescent of her right ear. Responding to Shelley's stare, she stuck out her studded tongue.

"I hope you don't mind my sitting here," Yasmira said. "Us women of color should stick together."

Yasmira had an exotic look of indeterminate origin, an olive-gray skin. Using her tiny pearly teeth, she ripped open one wrapper after another, liberating the saltines. She dumped them into her soup bowl, transforming the brew into a swamp of soggy wafers.

"I'm Shelley Krieg."

"Mira. In answer to your question, I'm from Libya, African-American and all."

In other iterations she would declare she came from Lisbon, Lebanon, and a small Greek island. Sometimes she was more directly oblique: "I'm Lisbyan" or "I'm Lesbanese."

"I'm not," Shelley said.

Mira tugged her unpierced earlobe. "Don't worry, I'm only 90% gay." Whenever she made one of her idiosyncratic jokes, Mira's lips drew back in a flat-line smile as she waited to determine whether the listener shared her odd sense of humor.

Shelley felt uncomfortable, certain Mira was hitting on her. Being tall and strong, Shelley had been called a lesbian and most of its cruder variants since her days as an oversized kid on the playground. Now, as a cop, she still got remarks from street hoods and snotty fellow officers. She had to wrestle with her history to separate *lesbian* from the realm of childish slurs.

"I'm not out to climb into your pants," Mira said, as though reading her mind. "Just being friendly." She shoveled a spoonful of cracker mush into her mouth.

Shelley soon came to realize that beneath her new acquaintance's self-mocking and in-your-face pronouncements, Mira possessed a charming sweetness and a playful spirit.

In her early days as a beat cop, Shelley was as strait-laced and uptight as they come. Mira represented escape. They hit the bars together, saw theater, undertook regular excursions to the Kennedy Center, shared secrets, and exchanged late-night phone calls when they read aloud and snickered at *Cosmopolitan* advice columns.

One night, at two A.M., Shelley answered a call from Mira, who begged her to come over right away, to help with an emergency. "I need you to play police officer, Shel."

"*Play?*"

"I need your domestic-dispute personality. To calm things down."

When Mira's lover threatened to walk out, Mira had panicked and snatched her car keys.

"She says she's going to report me as a car thief," Mira told Shelley over the phone, sobbing. "This'll ruin my career. I'll lose my job."

"Just give her the keys," Shelley said.

"I threw them down the sewer drain."

When Shelley arrived at Mira's place, Mira met her at the door. "I need you to pretend to write up her complaint, like you were a real cop."

"I *am* a real cop."

"You know what I mean." Mira winked.

Shelley marched into the bedroom. Leather straps and fur were strewn about the bed. She informed the girlfriend, "Mira tossed your keys into the sewer. She is going to pay to make new keys for your car."

"Just get a locksmith to open my apartment and I can get my second set," the girlfriend said.

"Deal," Shelley replied.

"And make Mira swear she'll never call me again."

With Mira short on cash, Shelley floated her a loan to pay for an all-night locksmith and a taxi. The ex-lover slammed the door on her way out.

Shelley was furious. Mira had violated their friendship by using Shelley as her personal policewoman.

Mira acted as though all was normal, just the end of another ladies' night out. This enraged Shelley even more.

"Jesus—what do we really have in common, anyhow?" Shelley had said. "How dare you drag me into your freak show."

Mira appeared oblivious to the insult. She looked up at Shelley with wide, reverent eyes.

For the first time Shelley had recognized how much of their relationship was based on worship—and how much Mira fed her ego. Her friend was just another tall-woman fetishist, a height-hound. Soon Shelley began begging out of get-togethers, inventing excuses.

Before parting that night, they agreed not to speak of the key-napping incident to anyone. "I owe you big time," Mira had said. "Anything short of murder."

10

MIRA ARRIVED WEARING a conservative business suit over a white shirt with ruffles. Gone was the cascade of piercings along her ear. She could have been a real estate agent showing a house.

She reacted to the butchered body with a remarkable degree of coolness: a simple frown and a tilt of her head. She readily accepted Shelley's story, how she had woken in a daze, found the victim, heard whispers, and felt the breeze coming from the bathroom; how she had charged in there only to be knocked out cold.

"I need a second set of eyes," Shelley said. "A second brain. I need you to help me think about how this happened. Why, who, whatever. I'm both victim and detective and that can screw with my objectivity. The moment I report this body, the case will get pulled from me. Before I do, I need to copy the Raffi files. I'm heading to HQ."

"So I get to babysit a corpse? Cool. But I'm not going to burp him."

Mira had picked up her often-macabre sense of humor in her job as a senior technician at the crime lab. Although an abstract gruesomeness underpinned many of the samples Mira processed, she wasn't experienced with visiting crime scenes or viewing the grisly results of violence.

Despite the fact that Mira seemed calm, Shelley recognized a twitch of nervousness beneath her friend's façade. "This could be dangerous," Shelley said. "I'm worried the moment I'm seen at the station, someone will think they can march back here for a visit. I need you to stay here, to scare them off, to call me. As an officer, I'm not supposed to do this, but you need this more than I do." She offered her gun to Mira.

"Jesus!" Mira said. "No guns. You've heard that statistic about how guns are ten times more likely to kill the owner than the burglar? That's because of people like me. I'd shoot myself in the foot and face before hitting anyone else."

"It has only one bullet. So you'll have to choose between your foot and your face." When Mira continued to look horrified, Shelley said, "Seriously, I'm not telling you to shoot anyone. Just use it to make noise. Scare the intruder away." She set her gun on the dresser. Mira covered it with a pillow.

"It's there if you need it. Just as a back-up plan," Shelley continued. "This neighborhood is tight. We look after each other so I can't imagine anyone trying to break in, in broad daylight."

Mira beamed a smile. "Thanks, Shel."

"Thanks?"

"For making me the go-to person you'd call."

Shelley studied her friend. Mira offered up an adoring look as though the last two years of distancing had never happened. Shelley felt a twinge of guilt for getting her friend involved.

"Thank *you*, Mira. There's no one else I can trust with this."

The words hung silent and awkward for a moment. Shelley's voice dropped an octave; her tone became solemn.

"I met a man last night."

"You sound so serious. Was he that bad?"

"Maybe. I'm thinking ... when I woke up I felt disoriented. He bought me a drink a little before midnight. I think he might have drugged me."

Mira put on her forensic scientist's face: clinical, but with an underlying concern. "Only one drink?"

"Yes."

"He didn't come home with you?"

"No."

"How long between the drink and going to bed?"

"About an hour and a half."

"During that time did you feel light-headed? Wobbly?"

"No. Just a buzz from the drink."

"Then it didn't happen," Mira concluded. "There are time-release pills, but once they dissolve they start working. There's no such thing as a delayed-action drink."

Shelley sighed in relief.

"Is he cute?" Mira asked.

"Very." An involuntary smile spread across Shelley's lips. She fought it back. "Um ... Mira? I thought I'd been drugged, so I saved a cup of pee in my fridge. Just in case you wonder what's in that jar."

"Good to know."

"I've got to go. Keep safe and call me if anything comes up." She slid on a jacket and grabbed her pocketbook.

"Shel? You can't just leave me hanging without letting me in on the plan. What are you going to tell them about the body?"

"I'll call this in when I get back. I'll tell them when I came home last night, I slept exhausted on my sofa. I didn't discover the body until I returned this afternoon."

"And how did you get dressed without going to your room? You're claiming you saw no signs anyone broke in? When you took a shower, you didn't notice the broken window?"

"You do a good drilling," Shelley admitted. "I'll work on my story."

Mira stretched her arms overhead, let out a whistle, and plopped backwards onto the bed—just an arm's length from the cadaver on the floor. She stretched, wriggled to settle in for comfort.

"Why are you doing this, Shel? You know if we get caught in this cover-up, we're both out of a job. Obstructing justice. Maybe jail time."

"I have to get hold of the files. I can't let them railroad Raffi."

"You told me that already."

"Look, the only ones who know what took place here are the killers and I doubt they'll be fessing up. When I get to the station house, I'll act like nothing happened and see if that makes someone edgy. You cool with this?"

"Okay. Look, Shel, I realize this is NMS but I can handle it."

"NMS? Raffi used that same phrase. What does it mean?"

"Not mind safe. When what you encounter is just too much to wrap your head around. But I'll be fine. Maybe I'll take a Xanax."

"Since when do you need Xanax?"

"Since I started getting panic attacks. Of course, most of the time my panic comes from wondering, where's my Xanax?"

Shelley glared at her friend.

"I'll be fine, Shel. But you still didn't answer my question. Why risk everything for this kid?"

Shelley answered, "Because of the worst person in the world."

11

WHEN SHELLEY BEGAN the fourth grade her parents allowed her for the first time to walk home from school without adult supervision—providing she did so with a band of her school-mates.

She took her new privilege seriously, policing her friends, ensuring they huddled together and crossed streets only at designated crosswalks.

One day a homeless man, whom the kids called "Stinko," followed their group from a distance.

The kids yelled at him, telling him to go away. When he didn't, they picked up wood chips from a nearby garden and chucked them at him. He ducked behind a tree but still wouldn't retreat.

As they continued to hurl wood chips, Shelley's father pulled up in his Taurus.

"What's going on here?" he demanded.

"It's Stinko!" Shelley said. "He's chasing us. He's hateful!"

"Just a moment." Her father walked up to the man cowering behind the tree trunk. They exchanged words in low mumbling tones. Then her father returned with a Hello Kitty notepad cupped in his palm.

"One of you dropped this," he said.

A girl stepped up. "Thank you, Mr. Krieg."

"I want to talk with my daughter," Krieg said. When this failed to break up the group, he added, "Alone."

The other kids slinked away.

"Stinko didn't have to scare us," Shelley said. "He could have waved the notepad and put it on the ground for us to pick up."

Mr. Krieg took his daughter by the shoulders and locked eyes with her, making sure she could not look away. "His name is not Stinko. He's Dell. Delbert Lyons. When we were young, he was my friend. I don't know what makes some folks go crazy, but when Dell was about twenty he started cutting his arms with glass and shouting at people even when nobody was around. It's not his fault he is how he is. I want you to tell him you're sorry you threw things at him."

"I'm not sorry."

Her father sighed. He said, "Let me tell you a story about the worst person in the world, Shelley. When I was young, I mean about thirty, I saw this homeless lady. Unbathed, stringy hair, dirt lines so deep they seemed scratched into her face. She came up to me and begged me for money in this desperate, rasping voice. She raised up a palm already full of coins. Something about how pathetic she seemed made me give her six quarters. All I had for the bus."

"And she was the worst person?"

Mr. Krieg ignored his daughter's question. "When she got the money from me, she headed over to this thug. He was holding a loaf of bread in one hand, held up high. She showed him her coins. He grabbed her by the wrist and twisted so that all the coins fell to the pavement. He refused to give her the loaf of bread and told her to bring him more money."

"And he was the worst person in the world?"

"Standing not far off, there was this police officer. He saw everything and he just laughed." Before his daughter could ask again, he answered her, "No, he was not the worst person. While all of this was taking place, I stood there and I did nothing. I was the worst person in the world."

Shelley's eyes teared up.

"Sometimes," her father said, "you see a wrong. You see someone weak who's got no one out there to help them. That's when you've got to stand tall."

12

WITH MIRA GUARDING the house and its secret, Shelley backed out of her driveway and began driving down the short loop of her street.

She lived in her parents' old house in the eastern corner of DC in an area called Lincoln Heights. As her older siblings came of age and got married, one by one, they had abandoned the neighborhood, choosing the suburbs as the place to raise kids. Then, when her father passed away nine years back, her mother moved to Atlanta to care for her older sister. Shelley stayed in the house, a one-floor affair with a nice yard and a two-car garage. Its cellar, as wide and as long as the house, had a door to the alleyway. For years, her family had considered converting the space into a basement apartment. For now, though, it still functioned as a warehouse for the junk, furniture, and bric-a-brac that had never found their way to Goodwill.

Lincoln Heights had been Shelley's home her entire life. She knew everyone, all of them hangers-on who, like herself, refused to abandon their turf even in the face of encroaching blight.

To get to the precinct headquarters, she took East Capitol Street across the Anacostia River, a straight shot aiming at the giant dome that housed Congress.

The power center of the nation's capital made for fine eye candy, an Emerald City of manicured lawns rolling out like royal carpets between the marbled monuments and an alphabet jumble of national institutes and post-colonial buildings. Other avenues featured crystal offices interspersed with overpriced restaurants whose prices were affordable only to lobbyists baiting their hooks. To Shelley, these aspects of Washington felt like background noise; they had nothing to do with the grit and black beauty of the community she loved. A full half of the District's population was African-American. As a Southern-Northern city, DC was steeped in a history of segregation and civil rights. Its natives projected a defiant pride to all who viewed it only as a maze of bureaucracy or as a national podium for windbags. To Shelley, this territory where poverty cohabited with ravishing beauty would be forever her home.

The Third Precinct headquarters was located on V Street in a neighborhood made up of row houses owned by urban homesteaders, second-generation immigrants, and a smattering of longtime residents. The police building looked like a dull brick schoolhouse, two stories tall, its length stretching across five banks of multi-paneled windows.

Before entering, Shelley smoothed her blouse and slacks and wiped the moisture from her palms on the lining of her pockets. *Nothing unusual has happened*, she told herself. *This is an ordinary day.*

She took the officer's gate, bypassing the metal detector. As she pressed the elevator button for the second floor, Click Morretti slipped in beside her.

The slowest two-floor elevator ride on Earth has just become the most torturous, she thought.

"You look like crap," Morretti said in greeting.

"And you look like no-shit, Sherlock," Shelley replied.

"You're running that joke into the ground, Krieg. Pretty soon it won't even be able to hurt my feelings anymore."

"I'll tell you why I look like crap. Last night I fell asleep on my living room sofa."

"You did?"

"Never made it to my bedroom."

"Uh-huh." He offered a confused scribble of a smile. "Good to know."

The doors slid open and Morretti swung his arm out, inviting her to go first.

"Welcome to the shitstorm," he said.

A wide room extending the length of the second floor made up the detective division. Along its sides were offices, cubicles, and the observation and interrogation rooms. In the center, desks were peopled with faces well known to Shelley, along with a few unfamiliar faces. She saw Atch, Jones, Kaufman, and Slatterly from the weekday squad and some of the week-end crew. Kent was MIA. Tate's jowls waggled as he chatted up a young female detective.

Shelley scrutinized Atch and Click. Someone with police savvy had killed Cassidy, but try as she might, she couldn't imagine them as butchers.

She scanned the other faces, wondering who-all might be cold-blooded killers. She had hoped someone would react to her presence. What did she expect? A flash of fear, a jaw agape? A supervillain chortle? Instead some, but not all, stared at Shelley as though she were one of the walking dead. They knew something she didn't.

Tate caught sight of her. He broke from his conversation and called out, "Listen up! Lieutenant Krieg, the primary on this case, has joined us." Mutters became whispers. "As most of you know, we booked Rafael Hooks last night for the murder of his brother, Keshawn Davies. At the time we believed Hooks to be nineteen, mainly because of his driver's license. He is sixteen and a juvie. According to his lawyer, he obtained a fairly convincing fake ID so he could acquire his own apartment."

Shelley pinched her forehead.

The captain continued, "Because Mr. Hooks is underage, a juvie officer should have been present during questioning. Short of that, when he asked to see his mother, one Esmay Hooks, his request should have been respected and the interrogation should have been delayed."

"You gave me his age," Shelley whispered to Click through gritted teeth.

"And you could have checked it out," he whispered back.

He was right. She should have inspected his ID close-up. She should have run the info through DMV.

"Consider the entire interview as tossed, invalid," Tate said.

"It had good faith written all over it," Shelley protested.

"Be that as it may," the captain said, "it gets worse. While in adult lock-up, his fellow detainees welcomed Hooks with a greet and beat. The bruising was substantial. His injuries would have been worse but, to Mr. Hooks' good fortune, the error in his incarceration had just been discovered. When a sheriff and corrections officer arrived to transfer him, they halted the attack in progress.

"Rafael Hooks now resides in the Corrections Facility Hospital. In spite of being the prime suspect in two homicides, he has announced a civil suit against the department along with separate suits against Sergeant Bellotti and Lieutenant Krieg. With his confession off the table, come Monday, a bleeding-heart judge might well cut him loose. We need to explore new directions to make a case. Detective Krieg will lead the effort to undo the damage she caused." Tate turned to Shelley. "Detective Krieg, I want a report on what went wrong, an assessment of the state of the case against Mr. Hooks, and an item-by-item list of assignments to hand out along with recommendations of how to make this case stick. When we prove he is the killer, his lawsuit will lose traction."

Most of Krieg's fellow officers recognized her competence and looked to her with sympathy. Those who considered her arrogant, including Morretti, tried to contain condescending smirks.

"Detective Atchison," Tate went on, "in the absence of Bellotti, you'll run second on the case."

"Captain," Atch said, "Morretti and I caught the call and visited the scene. Under the circumstances, Krieg should be sidelined while we play lead."

"Command is slow-roasting my rump," Tate said. "They've asked me to sever Krieg from the case. But I'm not about to bury her before I review her report. Still, Lieutenant, you do have a point." He shifted his line of sight from Atch to Shelley. "Detective Krieg, cc Atchison and Morretti on all you do. Make all of your decisions, joint decisions. There's a good chance this will be their baby soon. As for anyone not on assignment, make yourself available to Krieg. We'll meet on this again in an hour after I can sort through Krieg's recommendations and parcel out further assignments. That is all." Tate headed to his office.

Morretti expressed his distaste for the pecking order with a lip-sucking frown. "You write the reports," he told Shelley, "and let us pros do the investigating."

"Where's the case file?" Shelley asked.

"My desk," Atch said. Morretti jerked a thumb, signaling to Atch to join him, to pow-wow in private. Together they ducked into a cubicle.

WITH THE HELP of the royal fuck-up, the case folder had grown remarkably thick overnight, having swollen to over a hundred pages: a report from the corrections officer, the sheriff's official report, a medical intake sheet, photos of Raffi's recent injuries.

There was a blow-up of the phony ID in question; the last digit in the year of birth had been changed. The re-lamination of the card appeared sloppy and amateur.

Along with the original reports from Shelley and Kent, the file contained statements from Click and Atch. She flipped through Morretti's statement. No mention that he'd been the one who'd announced the kid was nineteen. *Asshole.*

On a transcript of the interrogation, all appearances of the word "mother" were highlighted in yellow.

The case folder also included dozens of photos of the crime scene and the victim, Keshawn Davies. Shelley needed to study these.

She collared a secretary. "I need a photocopy of every page of this file. And a color copy of each of the photos."

The secretary wrinkled her nose. "The color machine is out."

"Then take it to Kinko's."

"Not part of my duties."

"Do you like your job?"

The secretary cocked her an evil eye. "It's a job."

"It won't be if you don't get moving." Shelley counted out four twenties, placing them in a line on the desk. "For the taxi, the copies, and the trouble."

The secretary scooped up the bills. Rising to her feet, even though a full head shorter, she stood toe to toe with Detective Krieg. "Don't you ever bully me. My union is every bit as good as yours." She grabbed the folder and left.

Shelley knew the secretary was right. She had absurdly escalated the matter, threatening the woman's livelihood. She would apologize—later, when she returned to sanity.

For now, she stepped into the ladies' room, where she splashed cold water on her face. She inspected her reflection, shocked. She thought she'd been putting up a good front: unflustered and self-assured. Instead, she looked like crap, a wild-eyed corpse kept in motion by caffeine. She massaged the ridges beneath her eyes, trying to wring out the exhaustion. She pushed the heels of her hands against her eye bulbs. They responded with a dull pain and bursts of color beneath her closed lids.

Before leaving the bathroom, she rehearsed a tough and confident smile in the mirror until she nearly convinced herself. *Good*, she thought. *I'm ready. Look out, fuckers. I'm coming for you.*

13

SHELLEY REENTERED THE detectives' floor with its long garden of desks. With the captain's speech finished, the underlings had returned to their paperwork and cubbyholes. At the far end, Click and Atch chatted it up with a pair of Prince George's detectives. She watched as they dragged chairs into an interrogation room.

Damn! Shelley thought. *The Ernesto Grey murder—that's my interview.* She stormed across the room. As she made ready to swing open the door to interrogation, she paused. *Wait ... why not listen to them from observation?* She could find out whether Click and Atch were undermining her investigation. Maybe she could get them bumped from the case.

She entered the slender slice of room behind the two-way mirror. Before switching on the speakers, she studied the detectives. Morretti's shoulders were hunched up, his chest and stomach bulging out of his jacket. His bright yellow tie was an offense to the eye: It looked like a giant mustard streak smeared from his chin to his belly. Mannered and snooty, Atch sported a chiseled haircut, bleached teeth, manicured nails, and perfect posture. The hem of his glossy silk shirt lay tucked under the slim waistline of his perfectly creased pants. Morretti and Atch—the unoriginal Odd Couple.

Click directed the conversation, waving his hands, tugging on his sleeve, and pumping his fist. Atch clenched his teeth as though he was suffering through the same joke for the thousandth time. He probably was.

Two PG detectives listened to Click with polite, gritted smiles. One appeared to be in his mid-thirties. He wore a sergeant's shield, Mt. Rainier PD. African-American, compact, and muscular, he kept his head shaved. It seemed as hard and smooth as a crash helmet. He would have made a decent human cannonball.

The other Maryland detective was a white male, ghoulishly pale and somber, in the middle of middle age. He sported a lieutenant's badge: Narcotics. It appeared that he had once been fit and well-toned, but now his muscles drooped after exchanging weightlifting for pencil-pushing. An empty plastic protector lined the pocket of his dress shirt. He leaned back, tipping his chair. His tie wagged to the side.

When Morretti's joke ended, the faces turned serious. The members of the cabal leaned nearer to one another.

Shelley flipped on the monitor. Morretti was speaking. "For the time being we'll have to cut down on the snitch-snatch."

"I hear Kent's been getting some epic pussy," Atch said.

"Really?" Click said.

"His babysitter."

Click made a circle with his lips. "Ooh, that little hell-raiser. My respect for him just jumped twentyfold."

"What about Krieg?" the older detective said. "Can we rely on her?"

Click reacted with horror. "About as much as I'd trust a shark to give me a blow job."

Shelley's cell phone chirped. Although the observation room had soundproofing, she had left the side door open. She imagined the noise traveling into the office space and under the interrogation-room door. Click's eyes flashed in the direction of the mirror and then quickly looked in the other direction.

Ah, hell, I'm going in. Shelley turned off the speaker, looked to her cellular for the text: "CQRT = INCQRT. DITYID? HB. M." Shelley racked her brain to translate this gobbledygook. She got only as far as "Hurry Back. Mira."

Shelley quickly slid past the door to the interrogation room to pretend that she was casually approaching from the other direction. The door swung open. Click poked his head out. He mimed holding up a bullfighter's cape, pulling it back to let her pass, then he hustled out to scrounge up a fifth chair.

As Shelley entered, the two Maryland detectives rose, offering their hands.

"Jess Usher, NED, Major Case Section," the older man said.

"Shelley Krieg."

The shorter black detective cocked back his head as though he had to stare at the ceiling to take her in. A grin peeled back his lips. "Duggan. Call me Hap. Mt. Rainier PD." He rattled her hand.

"You know, you're sort of a legend in the Maryland force. We've got a name for you."

Shelley braced herself.

"Wonder Woman."

"I can live with that. Even though I know it's a kiss-ass lie."

"The best kind of lie."

Click returned with a chair and they all sat.

Shelley took charge. "The Keshawn Davies murder has a number of peculiarities. I'm told you caught a similar case in Maryland just over the District line."

"Your captain faxed us your report," Usher said. "Not much in common. Both had their chests chopped open rib by rib. Our stiff kept all of his fingers. No signs of torture. The murder took place out of doors. No marks suggesting a gag."

"Rafael Hooks knew both victims," Shelley said.

"True enough," Usher agreed. "And that's a major reason why we're here."

"But that only came out as part of the interrogation, which will probably be tossed," Duggan said.

An uncomfortable moment passed. All eyes locked on Shelley.

"Let's start by going through the Maryland crime," she said.

Usher nodded. "I found the body." He took out a clipboard, flopped over a few pages and began reading. "At zero-two-forty, Tuesday, October twenty-second ..."

"I can read the report," Shelley said. "Tell me the story as it happened and fill in what you left out of the write-up."

Usher puffed his cheeks like a blowfish, then blasted out a breath. His heavy lids drooped so that his eyes became slits as he dipped into the well of his memory. He said, "Ernesto Joaquin Grey, aged twenty-eight ... aging no more ... had worked as a freelance chemical peddler for going on eleven years, a confidential informant of mine for half that time. He's been a source of choice bits of intel that have netted my department at least ten prime busts. As far as I'm aware, up to this point, no one put a finger on him as a snitch and none of the dealers wised up as to who ratted them out. Looks like that might have changed.

"Tuesday, late night, two-forty in the A.M., he called me at home insisting he had a hot tip and asked me to meet him near the Mt. Rainier Public Works building, just off the railroad tracks and two long blocks south of Rhode Island, a spot we'd used for rendezvous in the past. He set the meet-up for three A.M. I asked him if what he had was worth me losing sleep. He answered, and I quote, 'Oh, mos def.' I got dressed and geared up. I arrived late, at three-ten. I hung around for about twenty minutes, suspecting a no-show. Then, as I started to leave, I noticed a pair of cowboy boots peeking out from behind a dumpster. Upon closer inspection, I encountered Ernesto connected to those boots. He was on his back, his chest cracked open and his ribs clipped. Loads of blood, a minor lake, told me the crime took place on site."

"Any other injuries?" Shelley asked.

"No. No signs of beating or even bruises from restraint. In fact, I described him in the report as peaceful-looking, as though he'd just decided to lie down and pop open his chest. The killing was recent. With the chill of the night, the blood from his wounds still gave off steam. I took out my weapon, inspected and secured the proximate area. Finding no immediate threat, I phoned in the crime. Call-in logged at three-thirty-two. Hap was assigned the case for Mt. Rainier PD and, because of my knowledge of the victim, I got sourced to play co-pilot. We've been running on the theory the killing represented payback from someone he'd ratted out."

"Cause of death?" Shelley asked.

"The ME said blood loss and shock leading to massive organ failure," Duggan said. "It seems you can cut open half a chest and still breathe from the other lung and keep your heart thumping. At least until the bleeding shuts you down."

"Drugs in his system?" Shelley asked.

"We're waiting on tox," Usher said. "Grey was a smack user. Considering the peaceful look on his face, I'm guessing he embarked on a chemical bon voyage prior to the butchering."

"Any particular physical evidence to indicate who else was there?" Shelley asked. "Footprints ...?"

"None."

"Did he call you from his cellular? Did you retrieve his phone?"

"He never carried one. The kid was paranoid, thought any-one could listen in. My caller ID showed his home number, a flop shack out on Highway One in College Park. He humped weed to the UM crowd."

Shelley closed her eyes and visualized the Keshawn Davies murder scene. "Did your lab match up the wounds to any special type of tool?"

"Nothing specific. The bones had been snipped, one by one, using top to bottom compression, not sliced through by a single blade. We were told pruning shears, bolt cutters, or a special tool that MEs and surgeons use to chop through ribs."

"Maybe the killer used some sort of barbecue equipment," Click said. He seemed serious. "You know, for divvying up a side of beef. For grilled ribs!"

"No," Hap Duggan said. "Butchers and slaughterhouses generally use meat saws or else manual or mechanical knives. A bit of trivia I picked up while working this case."

"Did you connect the MO, the chest carving, to any other crimes?" Shelley asked.

"Not in this neck of the world," Duggan answered.

"Meaning?"

"Nothing we need to concern ourselves with," Usher said.

His answer seemed a little too pat. Shelley let it go while making a mental note to check for herself.

Atch began nervously tapping the tabletop. He seemed un-aware of his action until all eyes turned on him. He silenced his finger. "So had you come across any leads that might connect Grey to Davies or Hooks?" he asked Duggan.

"Nope. How did Hooks know Grey?"

"A friend," Atch answered. "That's as much as he said before lawyering up."

"Did AZ ever come up on your radar when dealing with Grey?" Shelley asked.

"AZ?" Duggan responded. "He actually exists?"

"Grey never brought up that name," Usher said.

"Why do you think the killer cut open Grey's chest?" Click asked.

"I reckoned it was psycho revenge," Duggan said. "Old-World style. Now with two murders, I suspect serial psycho."

"It could be to send a message," Shelley said. "To spook others, to keep them in line."

"Spooked me," Usher said.

"This Rafael Hooks," Duggan said. "Only sixteen? So, he's like some junior-league Jeffrey Dahmer?"

Click bobbed his head. "He's got like this dead look in his eyes," he said. "No remorse. Scary kid."

Shelley wanted to spit.

"He's puny, doesn't look like he's got a single muscle in his arms. He's hardly some puffed-up goon. I doubt he has the strength to chop through bone."

"Detective Krieg," Usher said in a lawyerly tone, "are you stating you maintain misgivings regarding his guilt?"

Shelley bit her tongue.

"It won't be Krieg's case much longer," Click said.

"That brings us to reality," Atch said. "What's the game plan if this kid gets kicked?"

"We have to play on the side of public safety," Duggan said. He scratched at the blue fringe of the freshly shaved back of his head. "We'll rustle up an arrest warrant for the Maryland crime. Come Monday—if he's kicked—you arrest him, pending extradition. That'll hold him a while, probably time enough to build a case. Maybe we can get him locked up for a psych eval."

"You can get an arrest warrant?" Atch asked. "Maryland doesn't have jack on him for the Grey murder."

"With a little smoke and jazz we'll wangle a warrant," Usher said. "Just enough to hold him for a few days, keep him off of the streets while we rustle up the real goods. Our judges won't feel weighed down by the lawsuit baggage you've got hanging 'round your necks."

"I'd like to see your case file," Shelley said.

Usher leaned back and popped open his briefcase. He laid a thick rubber-band-wrapped manila folder on the table.

"We'd like to run off a copy of yours."

Shelley thought of the secretary. "I'll fetch it in a moment. And the C.I. jacket?"

Usher's face pinched. "Too volatile. It contains names of other confidential informants, intel on undercover operations. If you've got a specific question regarding its contents, I'll function as your eyes."

"We're running lab tests double-time here," Atch said. "Trying to dig ourselves out of this mess."

"I wonder ..." Shelley closed her eyes, projecting a mental image of her thoughts onto her eyelids.

"On the table in Raffi's apartment there was a notepad with some ink markings on it. Did the lab run an EDD for any letter indentations?"

"EDD?" Duggan asked.

"Electrostatic detection device," Shelley said. "It reads the words pressed into a page from writing on the sheet above. A fancy way of rubbing lead on paper."

"Nothing," Click said. "The pen had a felt tip. Must have been too mushy."

"Shel, if we're going to discuss our case, you should haul the file in here," Atch said. "Then we can study the two together, compare the wounds side by side."

Four sets of eyes waited on her response.

"Just a minute," she said, scooting back in her chair. Time to see if the secretary had returned.

OUTSIDE THE INTERROGATION room Shelley ran into a scowling Captain Tate. "Lieutenant Krieg." He spoke her name as though invoking a curse. "I gave you one assignment, prepare a report. Do not involve yourself further in this investigation until you've completed that task." He dropped his voice to a whisper. "I just got off the phone with HQ. They gave my backside another branding."

From the corner of her eye she saw the secretary drop a bundle of documents on her desk.

She considered her decision an easy one. As soon as Tate read her report he would manufacture a reason to relieve her of the case and then go dowse his rear end. If she took the blame for not determining Raffi's age, he'd use that to dismiss her from the case. If she tried to pass that off on Click, she'd be ducking her own responsibility and snitching on a fellow officer. Tate would certainly not approve of that.

"Captain, I didn't fully appreciate the heat you've been taking. As of this moment, I'm off the case. I'll prepare the report on my personal time, which you can start clocking as of now."

"You're bailing on me?" Tate asked. "After I stood up for you?"

"That sums it up."

As she turned her shoulder on him, Captain Tate grabbed her wrist. "What's with you, Shel?" he said. "Letting go of an investigation that wasn't ripped from your hands?"

They studied each other for a moment.

"I'm not dumb, Chief. I see how this is going to play. You plan to yank this case from me the moment you find something in my report to justify it."

"Fine, then. Walk away. Your decision. I'm placing an official reprimand in your jacket. Consider your weekend an unofficial suspension. As soon as you get your report on my desk I want you out of here."

"Yes—*sir*." She spaced the two words for maximum scorn.

She walked the original file package to those waiting in the interrogation room. "It's your baby now," she said, leaving the folder behind. "I've been given an involuntary holiday."

Three of the detectives frowned and offered consolations. Morretti said nothing.

SHELLEY SUNK IN her desk chair, considering her next move. Hunger banged on her belly. She fished through a drawer and encountered a half-empty can of sugar-powdered almonds. She downed them, then surreptitiously licked the sweet off her fingers.

She slipped the copied files into her briefcase, then unlocked her bottom desk drawer and took out her .38. She added this to her case, along with a couple of spare magazines for her .22.

She couldn't write the report at home. The moment she entered her house, it was going to be a crime scene. She grabbed hold of her laptop.

She tagged a note to her desk: *Gone to Starbucks.*

Before leaving the station she headed to the restroom, where she sat on a toilet, took a pee, and cried.

14

When Shelley was in her mid-teens, she hated being tall. Hated it. Susceptible to intense crushes, she felt powerless as her interests flitted from one boy to another. Whenever she tried to get close to them, they acted scared or—worse—amused.

Hunting down fashionable clothing of any kind in her size was a hard-enough endeavor, and then when she did find some, none of it appeared casual. She looked thirty and dowdy.

For a time, during forays beyond the boundaries of the neighborhood, when she passed among those who didn't know her, she took to wearing men's clothes. As a gangly tall teenaged boy, she didn't attract the stares and whispers. This period lasted until her boobs popped out. Then she realized that if she continued to venture out in men's clothes, she would look like a drag queen out of drag.

Come prom night, she wore a layered chiffon dress, specially designed and tailored to her height, expensive as hell, both elegant and immodest. She had an arranged date with a six-foot-five friend of her cousin. Then, at the last minute, he bailed out. His emergency replacement barely registered five-six. He spent the night pretending he'd arrived with someone else. She slipped out of the dance to cry alone in the back of her limousine.

There she received a glorious scolding from her driver.

"Why would you want to be ordinary?" he said. "Everybody, I mean everybody, will spend their lives looking up to you. You've got a gift and if others don't see it, I say shame on them."

He turned up the car radio and together they danced in the parking lot. He was old enough to be her father, but when they made slow turns to the golden oldies, she felt a sense of warmth and rightness. "Your heart counts most," he told her, "and that's where you're tall beyond measure."

At the evening's close, he drove her home and kissed her hand, saying, "Keep the faith, princess."

That night ended once and for all the feeling that she had to apologize to anyone for her height. Those who were intimidated by her—well, good. They should be.

SITTING ON A stool at the counter of a local Starbucks, with a fresh kick of caffeine in her system and a tuna-on-bagel sandwich in her belly, Shelley began furiously typing on her laptop. Her report didn't mention Morretti's announcement of

Raffi's age. She wouldn't rat on Click the way he'd sold her out. Besides, it had been her case and the buck stopped with her.

After reviewing the completed report, she couldn't miss the inevitable conclusion: Raffi was being railroaded and she'd been a part of it. As for Tate's requests for strategies to salvage the case, she had no intention of further helping them frame Raffi.

A small girl detached from her mother's side at the coffee line and walked up to her. "Do you play basketball?" the child asked.

"No," Shelley said with a smile, "I don't."

"How tall are you?"

"Six foot and then some."

The mother broke from the line to collect her daughter. "I'm sure this lady doesn't want to be asked these things."

"Coming from a child, it's sweet," Shelley said. "It's a little strange when adults ask me the same things."

"How can I be as tall as you?" the child asked.

"By listening to your mother," Shelley said.

The kid made a do-you-think-I'm-dumb face.

Shelley's phone rang. Mira. The mother took advantage of the momentary distraction to herd her daughter away.

"Shel, did you get my message?"

"You know I can't read that texting voodoo. Hurry back. That's the only part that registered."

"Jeez, Shel. It's simple. It said security is insecurity/Did I tell you I'm dying? When are you coming home?"

"I'm finishing up my report now. I'm off the case."

"Oh, wow. I'm sorry, Shel. But at least it means you can get your ass back here. Our friend is on top of a heating vent and he's starting to smell. The flies are having a party. Besides that ... somebody knows I'm here. Someone's been calling my cell. No talking, just hangs up."

"Keep the doors locked and the gun handy."

"It's in the freezer. I thought it'd be safest there."

"It's supposed to keep you safe, Mira."

A grunt.

"I'll be home in a bit. First, I've got a stop to make."

"Shel ..."

Shelley gave Mira a quick and distracted goodbye.

WITH HER REPORT complete and sent, Shelley headed to the DC Metro Central Archives to follow up on a nagging theory. Cassidy Higgins had served her as a police snitch. Ernesto Grey had done the same for Usher in Maryland. Maybe Ernesto had a DC record. A lot of criminals worked both sides of the border, playing catch-me-if-you-can between the jurisdictions. If Ernesto Grey did inform for the Metro PD, she could compare his files with Cassidy's to determine whether they had ratted out some of the same scumbags.

The Central Archives of the Metro police were housed just off the national mall in a modern glass building sandwiched between two churches. Shelley trotted up the archives' cement steps and entered. She presented her badge to the records clerk, who dutifully logged her in. To check out a confidential informant file, Shelley first had to fill out a request card, then wait for the clerk to enter it into a register, check her authorization, look up the file's location on the computer, and plunder the backroom to retrieve it. As a detective, Shelley's access to most records would be automatic. If access to a file was restricted, the clerk would inform her that approval from a superior would be required.

First, she asked for Ernesto Grey. The clerk notified her that Grey didn't have a C.I. file. In fact, he had no DC record whatsoever.

Next she asked for Higgins' C.I. file, passing over a request card. The clerk informed her that none existed.

"That's impossible," Shelley said. "I know Cassidy Higgins has a C.I. file. I've used him as an informant. Try looking up his general record, please."

The clerk typed the name into her workstation computer. "No Cassidy Higgins. No C.I. jacket, no record at all. Does he go by an alias?"

"I've retrieved his file before using this spelling, this name."

"I don't know what to tell you," the clerk said.

Finally, on a hunch that Davies had acted as a snitch, she asked for his file. Again nothing, not even a police report. He *had* been in the system. The records on Davies, Higgins, and Grey: all gone. Someone in the department was erasing his tracks and doing a damned good job of it.

SHELLEY HIT THE streets. Her mind buzzing, she drove distract-edly through midtown Washington. This being Saturday, the traffic was tolerable.

She thought back to her childhood. By age five, she'd already grown tall enough to board any roller coaster at the Six Flags amusement park. She blamed her amusement-park rush and too many police shows for her desire to be a cop. With their guns drawn, the TV police chased fleet-footed crooks through twisty alleyways, vaulting fences and playing Frogger with traffic. She envisioned life as a cop as a real-life shoot-the-chute ending in a takedown with her knee on the back of a captured perp.

Once she got a badge she learned that two-thirds of the job consisted of petty politics and filling out reports. Deathly dull, tedious, and annoying. Now, in a cruel irony, her job had become a thrill ride and she wanted off.

15

Mira answered the door, gun in hand. "The person calling my phone finally spoke. He said, 'Get out of the house, bitch.'"

"Okay, sorry. I'm here now."

"I thought this babysitting chore wouldn't bother me. It didn't at first. It was an adventure between friends, like I'd become part of your world again and why worry about Mr. Putrid? He's just dead. But he's not only dead, he's screwing with context. He shouldn't be here and now he's haunting your house with his funk."

"Mira ..."

"He's got flies on him. I thought they migrated south for the winter. Damn, I could use a Xanax."

"How many are you taking?"

"Too many yesterday, not enough today. That heavy-breathing SOB called me a bitch."

"The worst is over with," Shelley said. "I can take it from here."

"Shel, I've had time to think about what happened. How did they get into the house? You let them in. How come you don't remember? You were drugged. Not at the bar, in your house."

Shelley dropped into a chair. "That makes sense," she said. "It explains this pissy hangover."

"They doped you with something like a date-rape drug that wipes out memories. If it was GHB, it passes through the body quickly. You can detect it only if you take a urine specimen in the first ten hours. I can run the sample in your refrigerator at my lab."

Shelley envisioned her clock frozen at 3:38: the moment they cut the electricity. They must have drugged her moments before, when she opened her door and invited them in. *I turned off the alarm.*

"I can run the sample tomorrow. Sunday is practically a ghost town at the lab. GHB would explain why you and Raffi slept through the murders and don't remember a thing."

Shelley walked her fingers on the table. "We can't give the police the results from my sample. My entire invented story is based on sleeping the night in the living room and just discovering the corpse now. And it's too late to get a fresh urine sample from Raffi. But ... he pissed all over himself while waiting in the hallway after the arrest. Could you get drug residue from the clothes bagged in evidence?"

"It's possible." Mira thought some more. "More than possible."

Shelley shook her head. "Or else not. Tate passed the case to Atch and Click. It's not just that they won't listen to me, it's that they'll do the opposite. And they're working to hang the crime on Raffi, not prove him innocent. But there might be another way. While waiting for transport, Raffi peed on the carpet in the hallway of his apartment building. I'll bet it hasn't been removed as evidence. And the way they maintain that building, I guarantee it hasn't been cleaned."

"If we cut out a chunk of the carpeting, I can extract whatever residues it has. It should work."

"Okay, let's do it. This is an off-the-books operation, though. It won't net us evidence in the legal sense, but I can run the results past Tate to finagle an order to analyze the clothes. We'll go there tonight."

"Shel—you're forgetting about your houseguest. As soon as you call that in, they'll keep you on the hot seat for more than a few hours. And you'd better get a lawyer. I mean, I'm not sure I'd buy the story about how you're just finding the body now."

"If I tell them I came home and just found the body, I have to leave out being drugged. I can't use the evidence from my urine sample to help Raffi." She heard Morretti's mocking voice in her head. *The bigger they are, the harder they fall.*

"Shel," Mira said. "They wanted the corpse to be discovered here. Let's not play their game. Let's carry it off and dump it somewhere far away."

Shelley mulled over the idea. The notion was career-ending crazy. Risky and ridiculous. Most awful of all, it was the smart thing to do.

If she reported the body, she'd spend hours, maybe all night, at the police station. She'd be the target of a hundred probing questions and lurking behind those questions would be the reality that she sat on crucial evidence. She'd become part of the murder investigation, a bug under a microscope. Her home and her safety had been violated and a police inquiry would take away her only means of responding to the assault and humiliation, any chance she still had to continue her investigation.

If she couldn't collect and run the carpet sample, Raffi Hooks might rot in prison for a crime he didn't commit. Proof that someone had doped him with an amnesia-causing drug would validate his story. He could be freed without Shelley having to reveal her home invasion or explain how Cassidy came to be murdered at her place.

Dumping the body would allow her to erase all traces, to cleanse herself of the intrusion. She would take Cassidy to a place where he'd soon be discovered and given a proper burial. She'd leave a note with his name so he wouldn't languish unclaimed at the morgue.

"Sounds like we've got ourselves a busy night," Shelley said. She turned off her cellular. For the next few hours, she didn't want to be disturbed.

16

THEY STILL HAD hours before nightfall—time enough to carefully unmake the crime scene. Shelley and Mira both put on evidence gloves. Together, they ripped the cadaver from the blood that glued it to the carpet. Twelve hours had passed since the murder. Being over a heating vent had accelerated Cassidy's decay. The smell was horrid and rigor mortis had peaked, contracting his muscles and stiffening his arms, trunk, and legs. Cassidy had become as inflexible as lumber. They tugged a tall garment bag around his legs and torso and zippered him in up to his shoulders. Then they fitted another garment bag over his head. After scooting the makeshift body bag to the back of the closet, they tackled the chore of ripping out all of the bedroom's wall-to-wall carpeting.

"GHB and roofies are not magic," Mira explained as they worked. "I mean, some of the victims never recall a thing, but for others the memories return, bit by bit. You could have flashbacks. You might remember exactly what happened. At least up until the moment you blacked out."

Shelley rolled up the liberated carpet to the edge of the bed. Lifting together, they hauled the bed onto the denuded floor. Then they finished trundling the carpet to the edge of the wall, where once again they began to pluck out staples.

Shelley imagined the series of events. Three thirty A.M., she answered her door. Whom would she let in at that hour in the morning? The visitor invented some reason for dropping by, smooth-talking his way inside. Then he slipped her the drug. But how? At that hour of the morning, she wasn't likely to un-cork a bottle of wine.

Once unconscious, the others entered. How many? Two? Three? They carried her to her bed. She would have answered the door wearing her sweatpants. They must have taken them off her, rolling them down to their cuffs, the way she found them. She never left her clothes like that.

They cut the electricity. Why? To prevent the alarm from resetting. Probably first on their list after knocking her out. They needed the alarm off when they left. They lit the candle. To see what they were doing.

They brought in Cassidy. No signs of struggle on his body. Was he already drugged? Yes. Already dead? No, not dead. A lot of blood spilled from his body. They immobilized him with drugs, hauled him into her bedroom, and then butchered him.

They took apart her phone, tossing the battery into the cracked-open corpse, dropping the phone itself onto the blood-soaked carpet. They took the bullets from her gun and replaced the gun in the drawer. They wanted her up and about, dazed, groping around, contaminating the crime scene.

They broke the back window. To lure her into the bathroom. It was staged, the whole operation orchestrated to make her look equal parts suspect and incompetent. To have her repeat a lunatic story every bit as improbable as Raffi's. To get her off the case.

"GHB will make you woozy and forgetful," Mira continued. "But they probably gave you another drug. Something to knock you out quickly."

"Okay, so I might remember what happened. But do *they* know that? Unless they believe they've wiped out my memory for good, they might come back to finish me off."

"What do *they* believe? Hard to figure. I'm hoping they bought into the street myth that the drugs permanently erased their tracks."

17

SOMETHING DUGGAN HAD said in passing gnawed at the back of Shelley's mind. When she asked about similar crimes, he'd replied, *not in this neck of the world.*

Shelley begged off the remainder of clean-up detail. After booting up her computer, she undertook a two-pronged approach to her research, formal and informal. First she logged into the National Crime Information Center and Narcotics and Dangerous Drugs Information System databases. When the official sources drew blanks, she tried Google, playing around with combinations of search terms including *murder, chest, ribs,* or *rib cage* along with *carved, cut,* or *cracked.*

She trudged past results calling up horror fiction and *Alien* fan-fic with monsters bursting out of torsos. A rapper named Scarface wrote lyrics about ripping open chests. In Russia, a mob enforcer known only as Josef mutilated bodies in this manner as part of his signature.

Not in this neck of the world. Shelley searched for more background information on Josef, clicking on Russian newspaper links, passing the Cyrillic through Google Translate. No photo, no last name, no age, just occasional vague and conflicting depictions describing him as anywhere from five-feet-five to six feet, with blond or black hair, muscular or bony, 25 to 45 years of age.

At last she came across a lengthy account. The story identified him as Josef Serov. He'd once served as head of a special military unit assigned to breaking up the frequent hostage crises perpetrated by separatist guerillas during the Second Chechen War. The story went on to declare that the Russian government had secretly deemed those hostages expendable, claiming the resources spent rescuing them only validated the terrorists' mission. Serov's task force was authorized to wipe out the hostage takers with no concern for those held captive. Serov had ordered the murder of all the witnesses to their brutal tactics, pinning the blame on the terrorists.

The article was an unsourced, hysteria-driven piece, leading Shelley to believe she had encountered the conspiracy-blog equivalent of Russian journalism.

Shelley had a friend at the *Washington Post* who worked the Moscow desk. Maybe she could help evaluate the news source or run down some more intel on Serov. As Shelley flipped open her cellular to call her contact, Mira walked up behind her, startling her.

"We're going to have to toss the carpet in a place far from the body," Mira stated matter-of-factly. "Too much chance it can be traced back to you. Maybe we can use it to wrap a large dead animal, to give a reason for the blood."

"Do you happen to have a large dead animal handy?"

"In the back of the pound they keep an area where they pile up the recently gassed. My lab had to sort through them once to search for a source matching some stray animal hairs we were processing—not important, it's a long story. Only, I'm saying, I know where to look and how to get in. We'll need bolt-cutters and they have a security guard."

"No! We're not running some dead-pet caper."

Shelley's cell phone rang. She looked at the ID. *Taylor Jackson Singer.*

With mixed emotions, she answered the call.

"Hi," Taylor said in his smooth voice. "Sorry to bother you. And this will be the last time if you don't want ..."

"No. I want. It's just, everything has been ... my life has been all kinds of frantic. Police business."

Taylor laughed. "I can imagine. It's just I had to follow up, hoping you accepted the apology in my last message." She had listened only to the beginning of that message and that much hadn't come across as an apology. "And I'm hoping to get you out of the house and out on the town. How's supper tonight, where we can talk proper?"

"No, not tonight, Taylor. Can we make it next weekend?"

"I'm out of town for a week come Tuesday."

"Okay, then," Shelley said. "We'll talk. We'll talk, soon, I promise."

"Are you okay? You sound ..."

"This just isn't a good time, Taylor. That's how it is with cops."

Taylor grunted. "Okay, you got my number," he said—not "goodbye." He hung up.

Mira clucked her tongue. "I see your goo-goo eyes. Girl, you got it bad."

"Why now?" Shelley pointed her finger at her temple as though it were a gun. She mimed pulling the trigger, her head dropping to the side, her hand drawing back in recoil. "Where are my pants?"

"Umm ... you're wearing them?"

Shelley returned to her bedroom, where she fished yesterday's slacks out of the hamper. In the back pocket she found the card. "Taylor J. Singer, Landscaping." Her earlobes tingled as she read his number.

Mira appeared behind her. She said, "Honesty is important in building a relationship. You should tell him you need help dumping a dead body."

"Ha-ha."

"Ha-ha?" Mira echoed the laugh with derision. "Mr. Loveboat isn't here helping you with your criminal career. But I am. Earth to playgirl, we've got a job to do."

Shelley sat on the corner of her bed. A burgundy stain marked where blood had soaked through the carpet to the floorboards. "I've got a throw rug in my basement. It'll have to do for now."

She considered the makeshift body bag in the closet. "The rigor mortis will keep the corpse stiff for another few hours, so we'll have to move him as is, a six-foot-long plank. I've got good trunk space with the back seat down. I've moved a mattress before. We'll wait for dark and then we'll drag him to the garage. We'll bundle him in cellophane so he won't leave trace evidence in the car."

Shelley studied the leaning tower of rolled-up carpet. Twelve feet long. "We'll have to saw that in half," she said.

Mira gasped.

"I'm referring to the rug," Shelley added, to Mira's relief.

18

SHELLEY HAD LEFT a trail of bloody footprints on the floorboards of her hallway when she attempted to confront her home's invaders. *Stupid, stupid,* she thought—and then cut herself some slack. *Oh, hell, I was drugged, not thinking straight.* She attacked the stains with a scrub brush and ammonia.

Mira had the idea to replace the broken back window using a pane from an eleven-by-fourteen picture frame. It fit well enough, leaving just a sliver of a gap at the top. In the absence of glazier's putty she secured the glass in place with toothpaste that she hardened using a blow dryer, a trick she had learned during her college days, part of an arsenal of quick-fixes used to win back security deposits.

Shelley sawed the carpet roll in two. One half contained a mess of blood and torn skin; the other remained free of human residue. At six feet long, each half was as unwieldy as the corpse.

The box of cellophane said one hundred feet and included a blurb boasting about the number of pork chops and casserole dishes it could cover. It made no mention of how many corpses. Shelley snapped on evidence gloves and went to work swaddling Cassidy's corpse, head to foot, creating a mummy in a see-through bandage. She slipped a crumpled scrap of paper on which she had written his name into his hand, then sealed his fist closed. As she stretched the wrap around his face she remembered when they were on the debate team together. She'd had a crush on him.

Darkness descended. Mira sat at the kitchen table reviewing the case reports. Shelley draped herself over her living room sofa, staring out the bay window at the neighborhood lights until she dropped off to sleep.

She woke two hours later to see Mira bent over the kitchen table. Mira had borrowed Shelley's father's antique desk lamp and set it squarely in the center of the tabletop while arranging crime-scene photos here and there, mapping them out, recreating the floor plan of Raffi's apartment.

"It's about time, Sleeping Beauty," Mira said.

"Give me a break. I slept only a few hours last night and half of those were sprawled out on the bathroom floor."

"Yeah, I've had nights like that." Having raided Shelley's liquor stock to calm her nerves, Mira exhaled a boozy breath. She pointed at a close-up of the victim's face. "See these bands?" She traced a line with her fingernail along the creases running from the corners of Keshawn's lips out along his cheeks. "They're uniform in thickness, straight edges. Note the circles where the straps branched out. Those are linking rings to connect the leather bands. He wore a ball gag, straight out of your friendly neighborhood S and M shop. All well and good but, by itself, a ball gag is not enough to quiet a scream."

Shelley refrained from asking Mira how she knew this.

"They would need to also stuff a rag in his mouth," Mira continued. "Most bondage junkies don't go there. There's too much risk of choking. However, what's key is not the *fact* that they used a gag, but *why*."

"They couldn't let the neighbors hear him."

"More than that. They could have prevented his screams with a quick kill. They didn't do that. They had to keep him alive, torture him, *and* not let the neighbors hear him scream. They snipped off finger after finger of his left hand. But look at the ink blotches on the tips of the thumb and index finger of his right hand. He was holding a purple felt-tip pen, pinching it hard because of the pain. The marker bled onto his fingers. They tortured him, forcing him to write something, something he didn't want to write. Some sort of information that made him willing to suffer through four snipped fingers before he gave in and wrote it down."

Shelley had become accustomed to the brutal sights of homicides. She'd seen people who'd died sucking a shotgun barrel, heads that kept only their faces with the back of their skulls blasted to kingdom come. She'd seen helpless old men beaten to death for their Uncle Sam checks, children tossed down the stairs. Horrific visions that sometimes replayed themselves in sweat-soaked dreams. But for some reason, these images of Keshawn Davies felt even more brutal.

Mira tried acting nonchalant, but the story told by the photos tweaked and twitched the muscles on her face. She continued, "Just as important as Keshawn's treatment is the fact that Cassidy *wasn't* tortured. They didn't need information from him. I think Keshawn wrote down Cassidy's name."

Shelley thought for a moment, Keshawn tortured, gagged, forced to write. A single name? No. The torture went on for a time. He wrote a list of names.

"We've got a photo of the notepad," Shelley said, thumbing through the paper copies until she found it. "Here. It was on the table in Raffi's apartment." On a yellow legal pad, ragged green stains marked where the ink bled through the missing top page. "Three lines, three names." She connected the dots on the first line. Sure enough, they spelled out "Cass Higgins." She studied the blotches of ink on the other two lines. Without knowing the names in advance, they were impossible to decipher. She had to figure out who they were. Cassidy was only the first victim—this was a hit list.

19

In her early years on the force, back when she rotated between evening and late shifts, Shelley had learned the night had many faces. First came the bustle of early evening, which slowly decelerated like the lengthening intervals between ticks on a wound-down clock. In these hours, the time between passing cars grew farther and farther apart. By early-lateness, eleven p.m., most people were holed up in their homes, many asleep, others hypnotized by their televisions or computers. Then came the desert hours, the province of nomads and partygoers, restless youths and insomniacs, and workers bunkered in their ever-lit oases. During the desert hours, only the occasional roaring engine or riff of raucous laughter disturbed the night's vast emptiness.

Shelley chose the sweet spot of just before midnight, when most prying eyes had gone to bed but when an occasional wayward bit of traffic could still prowl the quiet lanes without rousing much suspicion. If a patrol car did stop her, she would bluff her way out of the jam by showing her badge.

She bolted her father's Virginia boating license plate on top of her car's tag, sticking a swath of reflective tape over the word "Boat." If some cop ran her out-of-state plate, the too-short series of numbers would confound any DMV search. She backed up her Malibu into her garage and sealed it in, lowering the garage's rolling door. Safe from prying eyes, she popped the trunk and dropped the back seat. Returning to her bedroom, she heaved the Saran-wrapped corpse over her shoulder and carried him to the garage. Once he was in position behind her trunk, she set him on his feet, then tipped him over to horizontal. She lifted and slid him into the back of the vehicle. Mira marveled at her friend's strength, sang froid, and efficiency. Shelley returned to the bedroom and grabbed hold of the two carpet rolls, tucking one under each arm like logs set for a caber-tossing contest. She hauled these to the garage and shoved them into the back seat of the car. With the front seats pushed forward, all the objects fit. Shelley slammed the trunk hatch down.

The temperature had fallen. Shelley put on an old jacket. Mira pulled on a tight black sweater.

———————

Rock Creek Park runs from the northern peak of the District to the southern border on the banks of the Potomac, dividing northwest Washington in two. On the expensive end of town, near the Montgomery County border, a number of slender lanes jutted like the prongs of a barbecue fork into the park's wooded terrain. Two years back, at the end of Juniper Street, an abandoned mansion had burned down in a spectacular fire. It was now a brick shell lost behind an expansive front yard, shaggy trees, and overgrown hedges. Conveniently, its circular drive provided easy access and escape.

Shelley made a first pass, letting Mira out in front of the charred porch. Mira hugged herself; the frosty air felt like the mid-forties. She inspected the grounds by flashlight, searching for squatters, druggies, or adventurous teens.

When Shelley returned, this time with the headlights cut, Mira signaled "all clear." Shelley idled the car and popped the trunk. She tugged the stiff corpse to its feet, then secured it in a rigid embrace. Together she and Mira waddled to the cellar's shattered trapdoor, then tipped the corpse over; it made a clattering crash landing. Standing at the brink of the pit, Shelley whispered a goodbye to Cass.

Mira beamed her flashlight down the hole to grab a last peek while Shelley climbed back into the car. Flinging the passenger's door open, she began to inch the vehicle away. Mira got the message and scrambled inside, slamming the door behind her. Shelley drove at a steady brisk pace back to Sixteenth, the main artery. Once there, she turned on her headlights and joined the traffic traveling south.

20

SIXTEENTH STREET SHOOTS up like an oak from its roots in Lafayette Park at the front of the White House. Its trunk rises and divides northwestern DC in two, often demarcating a line between the upper- and lower-middle class. Along the way, it is adorned by national shrines, temples, and embassies. After midnight on a Saturday, Shelley's car was one of several on her segment of the road.

With her car corpse-free, she turned the heater on. Mira sat folded up in the shotgun seat, knees to her chest.

"Shel? I was thinking ..."

"Mm-hmm."

"Raffi got jumped on and trashed while in custody, in his first few hours. How often does that happen?"

"It happens."

"But what if his pounding was more than just bad luck? What if someone planned to kill him and he caught a break, getting rescued in time?"

The light ahead turned yellow. Shelley wanted to punch through, but she remembered the traffic cameras. She slid the car to a stop and said, "You have a point. What are the odds he'd take a beating like that, first night in? One in a hundred cases? A thousand? And now ..." Anger helped Shelley focus and assemble her thoughts. "Here's a theory. They tortured and killed Keshawn Davies, drugging Raffi, framing him for the crime. Then they tried to kill Raffi in jail. With their lead suspect dead, they'd end the Davies and Grey murder investigations. Loose ends tied up, case closed."

"Except Raffi survived and you went around announcing you didn't like the case."

"I hardly announced it to the world."

"Just in a cops' bar. So they had to get you off the case."

"Okay. Let's say they had to kill Cassidy because he was on the list and then someone recognized that he and I had a history. So they did it at my place to screw me over and, of course, to get me off the case. Or maybe they wanted Atch and Morretti *on* the case. They were there at the crime scene claiming they were up in rotation, whining when I butted in, saying 'We caught the call.' Or did they make sure they'd be there? Did they accidentally mess up the scene? That's amateur, even for them. Or were they purposefully smudging tracks and flushing away evidence?"

They turned east on U Street. The area, once burnt out and ravaged by decay, had blossomed into an upscale urban island after the arrival of a subway stop. They continued on U until they hooked up with Florida Avenue and then turned left, entering a residential area.

It was well past midnight, and pedestrians had all but abandoned the streets. A drug runner posted himself at a corner, ready to serve the drive-through traffic. A pack of teens passed, herding together for safety. Television lights danced through apartment windows.

Shelley pulled over in front of 324 Oakdale.

"Coming inside or waiting here?" Shelley asked as she slung her crime-scene satchel over her shoulder.

"That's a crazy bitch-ass question," Mira said. The street lamp overhead was out. "Damned if I'm braving this neighborhood by myself in the dark. You don't know how lucky you are. You have no idea what it's like to feel small and vulnerable."

"Not true," Shelley said. "It's a big world out there and I'm sure as hell not bulletproof."

The building's management had responded to the murder by installing a fresh lock on the front door. They might as well have done nothing. It was a spring-latch bolt with an angled edge that retracted with only a modest shove. A single overhead light and far-off emergency exit sign lit the tunnel of the first-floor hallway. To the side, the stairs. The crime-scene tape had been removed.

"You handle the flashlight," Shelley said, passing it to Mira. "Aim it where I point." She slipped her bag from her shoulder to her hand. They tramped up the shadowy staircase.

The second-floor hallway had been stripped of the carpet with its bloody shoeprints. However, the patch at the top of the stairs welcomed them with a faint scent of urine. Shelley opened her satchel, extracting and tugging on a pair of vinyl gloves. She took out an evidence bag and box cutter. With Mira illuminating the target with the flashlight, Shelley knelt down and stabbed the razor's point into the fabric, sawing through the material, trimming and freeing a piece. She bagged the sample and crimped the pouch's seal.

"Is that it?" Mira asked.

Shelley didn't answer. Instead, she pointed forward and marched down the hallway. Slabs of light stretched out from beneath doors; otherwise, all was dark. For a moment Mira hung back, hesitating at the top of the stairs. Taking a deep breath, she scampered along the hall, holding the flashlight in front of her. They stopped at the entry to Raffi's apartment. The door was still crosshatched by crime-scene streamers. Tape trailed down the door frame, warning Do Not Break This Seal.

"Kill the light, Mira. In this hallway it's as good as screaming to the neighbors."

Mira cut the flashlight beam.

Shelley stooped in front of the door. She ran her finger along the half-inch gap between its frame and the floor. Just as she suspected, there was enough space. After leaving, the killers locked up from the hallway and slid the keys back into the room. Upon waking, Raffi gathered the keychain from the floor and opened the door for the police.

Shelley tried turning the knob. Locked. She rattled the door to see if the bars were thrown on the other locks. They weren't. Only an angled bolt prevented entry. From her satchel she took out a swath of plastic carved from a soda bottle. First, she ran her box cutter down the sealing tape. Then she slipped the strip of plastic through the gap in the door and beneath the bolt.

"What are you doing, Shel?" Mira asked, puffing nervously in the dark.

"My job."

"You didn't warn me you were going to do this. Isn't this breaking the law?"

Shelley gave no answer. The door popped open.

21

SHELLEY STEPPED INSIDE the apartment. Mira followed and Shelley softly shut the door. The room seemed as black as a bottomless pit, shadows devoured by deeper shadows.

"This is so NMS," Mira said.

Shelley tried the light switch. Nothing.

"Turn on the flashlight, Mira."

Mira turned the flashlight on, flitting the beam around until Shelley's palm covered it and gently removed it from Mira's grasp.

"Mira? Just hug the wall and don't touch anything."

"Okay." Mira scooted back to get out of Shelley's way.

After the twin blows of the murder and the CSI visit, the apartment seemed ripped to shreds. The evidence techs had gouged the mattress and cushions, probably searching for drugs.

All the cupboard doors, even the refrigerator door, hung open. Round yellow stickers with numbers were planted everywhere, identifying splatter points and sites of evidence collection. A fluorescent spot of paint marked where the victim's head had rested.

"I've never really visited a crime scene," Mira said. "Don't they make a chalk outline?"

"Only in the movies."

Shelley spotted a sharp dent where the swinging doorknob met the plasterboard wall. The door had exploded open, the key still in the lock.

She first imagined that this had happened when Keshawn arrived. No. That had been a moment of calm. Raffi would have invited his brother in. Maybe Keshawn entered with a stranger, someone who slipped Raffi the knockout drugs. Or maybe Keshawn had been talked into doping his brother, and the killer had arrived afterward.

When Shelley closed her eyes to try to picture what had happened, her mind flooded with the sound of a door chime. That wasn't right; Raffi's door had no bell. Her skin prickled. This was from a memory, very early Saturday morning. She recalled hearing her own door chime. Her SpongeBob clock emitted a low hum. 3:36 A.M. The electricity was on. The intruders hadn't yet invaded.

The doorbell again. She saw herself rolling out of bed, grabbing her sweatpants from the chair and slipping them on. She moved toward her front door. A familiar voice spoke to her from her front step. She tapped numbers on her keypad, suspending the alarm. She glanced through the peephole, but in this memory no image appeared. She slid back her deadbolt and twisted the doorknob. When her door opened, she saw nothing but shadows.

"Shel? Are you okay?"

Shelley's mind returned to this apartment, to *this* crime scene.

"Yes, Mira. I'm fine. I had a flash of a memory, but nothing complete."

Refocusing on her present location, Shelley realized what had happened with the key. When the police arrived, the officer booted the door the moment Raffi undid the bottom lock.

She had cracked The Mystery of the Dented Wall. No help in solving this crime.

Shelley concentrated, trying to come up with a plausible scenario to explain the murder in this room.

Keshawn knocked on the door. Raffi invited his brother in; the killer was right behind Keshawn. No, not one killer, but two or more. The job was too much for one perp to handle. Raffi was drugged, knocked out cold, and set in his bed, the covers pulled over him—no blood splatters on his clothes or the inside sheets. The killers seized Keshawn and gagged him. They sat him in the chair, gave him a writing pad and a pen with a leaky tip. They ordered him to write. He refused. They clipped off his fingers, one by one. Keshawn held out, but not forever. When he finished writing, they drugged him so they could butcher him while still alive, leaving behind a big pool of blood.

Shelley's stomach clenched, acid rising to her mouth. She took a bitter swallow. Time to search for clues to confirm—or refute—her reconstruction of the story.

She trailed the flashlight beam along the floor. The sweeping line of light allowed her to trace the blood's starburst pattern. The spurts originated from a spot near the wall. At that site, dribbles of blood on the floor marked a square perimeter, the size of a chair seat. Shelley drew back a chair from beneath the table. Blood marked the seat's edges, the center being where Keshawn had been sitting. She dragged the chair to where the torture took place.

He had sat in this chair, back to the wall, while they cut off his fingers. How did they keep him there? The chair legs had scratch marks. The floor had scratches matching the chair's footprint. They had tied him to the chair. She'd have to check out the autopsy photos for bruise lines around Keshawn's ankles.

Shelley closed her eyes again, continuing to envision the crime. Snip. One fingertip lopped off. An eruption of blood. A muffled scream. They put something on his finger stubs to stanch the bleeding while demanding *Write down the names*.

No cooperation. Time passed, the wound clotted, and the mental torture built as Keshawn anticipated the loss of another finger.

He held out through four clipped fingers, so he must have cared about the information he withheld. These weren't just random drug dealers or rivals he'd be double-crossing. Friends?

"Shel?" Mira whispered.

Someone walked down the hallway. The footfalls stopped outside Raffi's door. Shelley cut her light, probably too late. A moment passed where all she could hear was her own measured breaths.

The person outside the door gave a snort and passed on. A dozen footsteps and the jingle of keys.

"A neighbor," Shelley said.

"He must have seen the cut in the seal. He's probably calling the police."

Shelley nodded. "Five minutes and we're out of here."

She shone her light at the sink. She tried turning on the faucet. The water had been cut. She peeked beneath the sink. Of course—the CSI team had disconnected the drain trap, probably looking for the missing finger.

Shelley looked in the refrigerator, its light off, its motor cut. No food, five warm beers. The freezer contained a slurry of melted ice cream sandwiches.

During her first visit she hadn't bothered to inspect the bathroom. *Why the hell didn't I? Oh, yes.* Click announced the 911 tape had a confession. Click, who claimed the suspect was nineteen. *Click, Click, Click.*

The medicine cabinet in the bathroom hung open. Several tubes of ointments and overturned empty pill bottles. She checked the labels. Ritalin, Ritalin, Ambien.

The Ritalin wound him up, prevented him from sleeping. He took Ambien for insomnia. The perpetrator gave him a knockout drug on top of the sedative—that explained why Raffi had slept until 1:00 P.M.

The shower drain was covered by a metal strainer. Shelley knelt down and tugged on it. It was screwed in place. Trapped in a hole was what looked like soap scum. Shelley felt it, a hard nodule. She recognized it as cartilage. This had to be where the killer cleaned the rib cutter; the kitchen sink had no spots.

A slap of the wind made the bathroom's small window shudder. A far-away police siren howled.

Shelley plugged her mind into north, south, east, west, gauging the distance: *It's on First Street, heading north.* Another precinct. If a car came hunting for them it would arrive from the west. Besides, a report of someone violating a crime scene wouldn't warrant a siren, just a knock at the door, some Plasticuffs, and the end of a career.

Shelley peered out of the bathroom window into the side alley. A lookout stood sentry in the shadows, gun in hand.

22

THE STRANGER STOOD in the alley, his figure eclipsing a basement light. A sleek silver line traced the edge of his silhouette. He appeared to be of average height, slender, and muscular. Shelley could see his head tipped back—he was watching her window. His arm ended in a block, the chunky shape of an automatic. In response to Shelley's appearance at the window, he dipped his head and stepped back into deeper shadows.

Shelley drew her gun and rushed into the front room, ordering Mira to follow her. Shelley flung open the door and stooped beneath the crime tape. From her crouching position, she directed her flashlight and weapon up and down the length of the hallway.

"What's going on?" Mira asked.

Shelley responded by slide-cocking her automatic. An unnecessary move, but it made a dramatic click-click, enough to convince Mira to stop asking questions.

"Leave this to me," Shelley said, and hurried down the hall to the back stairs.

In spite of the warning, Mira sprinted to catch up, leaving Raffi's door ajar. Together they scrambled down the staircase.

Shelley opened the back door and peeked into the alley. Ducking back inside, she pitched Mira her car keys and her satchel.

"This is serious, Mira. Head out the front. Take the car. I'll meet you at the corner of Florida and Fourth. There's a service station and all-night liquor store. You'll be safe there. It's only five blocks from here. I doubt someone on foot would head that way."

Shelley opened the back door once more, this time slipping outside. With her back pressed against a brick wall, she scanned the alley. She glimpsed the shadowy figure of a man about forty yards away. His arms hung loosely at his sides.

Mira backed down the hallway step by step. Then she turned and ran, exiting out the front, not stopping until she was safe inside Shelley's car.

Shelley stepped a bit farther out into the alley, her gun pointed down and resting against her thigh. Her target stood too far away to ensure a disabling shot: The Metro PD pistol range set its practice targets at 25 yards. She'd never shot a human being. Her mind filled with the images of bullet holes puncturing paper silhouettes: neat round perforations through stationary sheets of paper. Two-dimensional and static. And they didn't shoot back. Before confronting her opponent, she needed to know how he handled a firearm.

She slowly raised her weapon, drawn at arm's length, her elbow unbent, the gun's aim pointed off to the side. A street punk would react with panic. A police officer would crouch, locking his body into firing position to offer a small target. The man in the shadows mirrored her movement with a slow sweep of the gun so that it was raised but not directed at her. She lowered her gun. He did the same.

So the stranger was cool-headed and a professional. A shoot-out at 40 yards against someone trained with a gun? She nixed that idea, choosing instead a safer but probably futile course of action.

"Police!" she called out. "Toss your weapon aside and drop to your knees."

The man immediately slipped farther back into the shadows. By the time she could make out his image again, he had put ten more yards between them and was running away.

"Halt!" she cried as she began chasing him.

He bolted across Third Street and here she got her best look at him, even if it was only from behind. Blond hair, short and curly. A mostly slender frame with broad shoulders. Half a foot shorter than she was, making him about five-ten.

Across the road, the neighborhood had reclaimed a once-empty lot as urban farmland. Now, in late October, the crops had all been harvested. Illuminated by flood lamps, the garden's ragged dead vines crawled along the dirt. The twigs of crumbling tomato plants were secured by twist-ties to a miniature forest of spikes.

The stranger leaped against the chain-link fence that guarded the field, flinging himself sideways, up, and over as smoothly as an Olympic athlete. He disappeared among a forest of skeletal cornstalks.

Shelley ran up to the fence hands first. The fingers of one hand splayed and threaded through the fence's web of coarse wire. Her other hand slammed the mesh with the side of her pistol. She looked over the cornfield, its tawny reeds as tall as she was, a deep grove with a labyrinth of paths cast into shadows by the stark illumination. Distant stalks shook as the stranger moved among them.

Shelley ended her pursuit. She wasn't about to enter a maze just to stumble upon a point-blank barrel.

But would he shoot? He'd had a chance to trade bullets. Instead he chose to flee.

Who wouldn't shoot? A fellow officer? She didn't think so. Someone who strictly followed orders. Observe, don't engage. *Military?*

Beyond the shriveled crops, on the far side of the back fence, a large black truck stood idling. Tinted windows. No plates.

Shelley stood there in the cold, her breath steaming. Finally, she holstered her gun and headed off to meet Mira.

23

SHELLEY SPOTTED HER car idling at the corner of Florida and Fourth, parked in front of Tito's liquor store. Mira popped up the door lock and Shelley slid into the passenger's seat. "He's blond, medium height, in good physical shape—he sure can scale a fence. And he wields a pistol like he knows how to use one—as well as when not to."

"What was he doing there? Has he been hanging around the murder scene all this time?"

"Or else he's been following us. There was a black pick-up idling nearby, the big, growly kind. It may be circling the area hunting for us. Let's edge the car around the corner where we won't be so visible."

Mira shifted the car into gear, turning down a side street and parking in the shadows.

"I'm sorry I involved you in this, Mira."

"It's okay, Shel. It's just—intense."

For a moment, neither of them spoke. Then Shelley said, "We need to get out of this neighborhood before our stalker picks up our trail. We need to dump the carpets far from here. Let's take the Anacostia south of town."

Heaving a deflating sigh, Mira pulled the car out. After weaving through some side streets, they connected to First.

Shelley covered the heating vents with her hands, the warmth conducting into her bones and spreading throughout her body. She stared at the rearview mirror, checking for tails. The streets were empty; nobody was shadowing them.

"You know," Mira said, "we make a crazy-good team."

"Too crazy."

They connected with Third Street and dipped into its series of tunnels, which then disgorged onto the freeway. Even there, they encountered only a smattering of traffic.

"You know how to get to the National Harbor?" Shelley asked.

"Of course."

"That's where we're headed."

AT TWO A.M. Daylight Savings Time kicked in and the hour repeated. With the car clock synced to satellite radio, a signal arrived that automatically jacked the hour backward.

Shelley turned on her cell phone. Two missed messages. The first was from Kent. 6:20 P.M. She put it on speaker.

"Oh, Shel. Shit. Only now I just got in touch with the station house. I'd been ducking them all day but they kept calling like crazy. So I found out they yanked us from the case and hung us out to dry. So that's why you wanted me to come over. Hey, look, if you need me, I'll call up my babysitter. It isn't a school night and she can stay late. Give me a call."

"School night?" Shelley said. "Damn. I heard at the station Kent is banging his babysitter."

"Seriously?"

"Mira, I don't know what's serious, anymore."

The second message came from Click at 7:10 P.M.

"Hey, Krieg," he said. "Here's a heads-up. We've connected the two cases. Seems Keshawn left a crisp bloody fingerprint on the crystal of Ernesto's watch. This links Raffi's brother to the Maryland murder. We sold a theory of the crime to a Maryland judge, saying Raffi and Keshawn killed Ernesto. Then Raffi killed Keshawn because he was a witness. The judge signed off on an arrest warrant. We can hold Raffi as a suspect in a DC pen while we sort out extradition. Hope you're enjoying your holiday while we're here doing your job. B-bye."

Shelley spit out a *pfft*. "A bloody fingerprint? A *legible* bloody fingerprint on a watch crystal, which went unnoticed until now? Usher said the killer left no physical traces and suddenly they discover decisive evidence on the corpse's watch crystal. I don't believe it. What do you want to bet the print is from Keshawn's lost pinkie?"

"Jesus, Shel. That's sick."

"If it's the left-hand pinkie, then they planted the print on the watch after Keshawn's death. To arrange that, they'd need access to the Maryland evidence."

"And who got hold of the finger?" Mira asked. "Maybe Click pocketed it at the crime scene, figuring he'd use it to plant some evidence."

"They're digging their own graves with this. Falsifying evidence like that will come back to chomp them in the ass."

"Unless no one cares."

"I care," Shelley said.

"I mean, let's say they kill Raffi and the case is closed, then they're thinking no one's going to look closely at the details."

They were coming up to the intersection between the Anacostia Freeway and the Beltway. A sign read: Maryland Welcomes You. Enjoy Your Stay.

"We can't let them get their hands on Raffi," Shelley said. "If he goes back to prison they'll have a second shot at him. I'm not going to let Raffi die."

"Damn, you're sexy when you're on a crusade."

Shelley nodded. "Yes, I am."

"Only one thing doesn't fit. Why kill Cassidy in the same fashion if they just wanted to close the case?"

Neither had an answer to that question.

DURING THE ALL-TOO-BRIEF bubble that comprised the tranquil portion of her childhood, Shelley's father liked to take his family boating. Everywhere: bucolic lakes, Virginia parks, and, especially, along the Potomac. While slowly drifting down the wide river, drinking her mother's home-brewed iced tea amid the buzz and chirr of insects, the caw of sweeping birds, and the occasional thunder of airport traffic, Shelley had peered out at the distant banks. As a burgeoning explorer and cartographer, she had memorized its shore.

Away from the city crowds, a short distance south of the National Harbor, there was a pier used by the West Potomac Rowing Crew. At this time of night, the area, which bordered a park, was as dark and lonely as a site could be this close to the city. Under Shelley's guidance, Mira drove along a dirt road to near the water's edge. Then Shelley hauled out the carpet rolls, lugging them to the end of the pier and dumping them into the Potomac. With a splash and a farewell burp, they disappeared.

24

WITH THEIR ILLICIT cargo disgorged, Shelley restored the car seats to their regular positions and took the wheel for the drive home. At last she had leg room and with it came a feeling of deliverance. The radio played a jazz so mellow and watery she might well have been swimming in an elevator. Mira slept, her small figure bunched up sideways in her seat, her shoes on the floor mat. Her mouth hung open and she breathed with a heavy-throated purr.

Shelley had spent her entire life in Lincoln Heights. Set far from the money centers and hip neighborhoods of Washington, it had never been invaded by the young and rich. Most passersby considered its streets menacing, equating them with the nearby projects and stretches of rundown houses. To her it had always been a haven, the safest spot on Earth. She knew everyone and everyone knew her. She was the local lady giant.

Now, as she drove along a too-dark section of street that fronted her house, she felt that her refuge had been forever transformed, invaded—desecrated. She clutched her automatic as her garage door scrolled up. She drove inside and cut the engine.

She gave Mira's shoulder a gentle jostle. "Wake up, dreamgirl."

Mira's eyes popped open. "I was in the middle of the shittiest nightmare ..."

Shelley climbed out of the car. Drawing her gun, she said, "Before we head inside, I'm going to scout the perimeter to make sure we haven't had another break-in. You wait here. Keep your phone handy and if you hear me call out, dial 911."

Mira punched 911 into her keypad, leaving her thumb hovering over SEND.

Before exiting the garage, Shelley pressed the button to close the door, sealing Mira inside.

She scanned the length of the street for potential threats. One direction was wide open and well-lit. The other end was congested with shaggy trees and had a blown-out street lamp, causing the street's route to quickly vanish among shadows. She recognized all of the nearby cars with the exception of one, an Audi parked three doors down. Tinted windows. She memorized its plate.

She slipped sideways along the narrow path between the side of her house and the hedge that marked her property's border. She kept her back to the wall, her gun gripped in both hands. Here, her windows were barred so that no one could take advantage of the seclusion and shadows to obtain entry.

The border hedge stood tall and ragged. She imagined that at any moment an attacker might leap from its jagged recesses. "Come out, come out," she whispered. No, the bad guys do those stupid jump-outs only in video games and Bond films. Heading down a slope, she reached the rear of her house.

The alleyway, with sentry lights beaming from the backs of houses and over the entrances to garages, was better lit than the street. Shelley identified several sites that could serve as a nest for a sniper: crouching behind garbage cans, on one knee on the blind side of a derelict van, lying flat on a garage roof ...

This area rested below street level and here a seldom-used entrance led to her basement. Some spider webs lay strung across the borders of the door. These were intact, declaring the seal unbroken. Above, the first-floor windows appeared intact, including the recently replaced bathroom glass.

She swept along the far side of her house and returned to the front. The face of her house appeared friendly and inviting, its bay windows standing tall and wide. These were secure, divided into an unbroken metalwork lattice of diamond-shaped panes. Looking through the window she could see that the electricity remained on. The alarm light winked at her. Having satisfied herself that all other entry points remained unviolated, she needed only to check the front door.

A Douglas fir stood alongside the single step up to her front door's entry platform. Slender, sculpted, the fir's silhouette rose like a spearhead to the height of the house's gutter. The porch light cast the tree's back side into deep shadow.

A stiff object stood between the fir tree and the wall. A dark block, the figure of a man.

Shelley raised her gun. This shot would be point blank.

"Don't move," she said, and swung over to the intruder's flank.

She recognized her uninvited guest immediately: a corpse wrapped in cellophane. Cassidy had found his way back.

25

SHELLEY TAPPED THE remote for the garage door. It rolled up to reveal Mira, her arms folded against the cold.

"Jesus, Shel, is it safe? When I heard you say, 'Don't move,' I figured that counted double for me."

"Someone dropped off a gift."

Mira craned her neck and, when that wasn't enough, took a slow semi-circular path to the front door. Encountering the plastic-wrapped corpse, she cried out, "Shit!"

"Cassidy again."

"You shouldn't go naming them, Shel. That's why they follow you home."

"They must have tailed us to the dump site—and I let them."
She gave her key a twist and the door a shove. She punched in
the alarm code. "Help me drag him inside."

"Shouldn't we just find another place to dump him, and fast
... before morning?"

"No. This time they'll be ready for us. I'm willing to bet
they'll phone in an anonymous tip and we'll get pulled over.
And then how do we explain our friend in the back seat?" Once
again Shelley tugged on a pair of vinyl gloves and handed a set
to Mira. "At the rate we're running through these we ought to
buy stock in the company."

They walked the cadaver indoors, wrapping their arms
around its shoulders and waist and conveying it along as though
guiding a drunken friend. But Cassidy had changed from even a
few hours back. His fierce stench now assaulted their noses and
eyes. The odor poked at the back of their throats like a jabbed
finger. A viscous ooze seeped from his feet. Maggots dropped
along the entryway floor. The corpse buckled along gashes in
the plastic as though it had grown new joints. The rigor mortis
was wearing off.

Mira withdrew a slick arm, shaking her hand and wiping her
fingers on the plastic.

Shelley leaned the slumping body against the entry-hall
mirror. She went to her kitchen, pulled out the full sack of
garbage from her large-sized trash can, twist-tied it, then lined
the receptacle with a fresh bag. She then set the container in
front of Mira, asking her to hold it in place. Shelley gave the
body a bear hug, hoisting Cassidy up and dropping his feet
into the trash can. Then she dragged the body backwards to

the utility closet, where she propped him up against shelves of household cleaners. She blasted him with room deodorizer and insecticide.

Mira nodded her approval. "You know how those cheesy personal ads say they're looking for partners in crime? Well, you and I, we're partners in crime."

When Shelley didn't respond, Mira said, more seriously, "I have a friend who works in a funeral home. They keep body bags on hand, you know, for when they get scoop-up cases like shut-ins who rot for a month before someone discovers them. I'll bum a bag for you in the morning."

"Good, that'll work."

Shelley felt simultaneously exhausted and jittery. She needed to sleep but knew she couldn't. "Mira, we'll stand guard in shifts. I'll take the first watch. You catch a nap and we'll trade off in a couple of hours."

"Shel? Do you have other friends who might help us? I mean, it's nice being the one you go to for your *Breaking Bad* adventures, but it also kind of sucks. This started out freaky and it keeps heading farther off the deep end. Do we even have a plan for what we're going to do with old stinky?"

"Cassidy. His name is Cassidy."

"Oh, Cassidy! Don't mean to insult Mr. Putrid. After this, I don't owe you a thing. We're even." Mira pulled her sweater up over her head. "After this, you owe me big time." She cupped a bra cup in her hand. "Sweetest mini-tits on the planet." Then she announced, "I'm taking a shower and then I'm diving into the sack."

"'Night, Mira," Shelley said, but her friend had already trudged off, heading down the hall.

Shelley repositioned her father's recliner to face the living room's bay window. She rested her automatic across her lap.

Staying awake felt like a staring contest. Shelley's dry eyes burned. Still she maintained a fiery gaze out of the window, her teeth gritted and grinding.

The street scene was a vast display of monotony. Not even the flash of a headlight. She felt as though she might as well be staring at a museum piece, waiting for a portrait to crack a smile.

Plan. I need a plan, she told herself. *Here's the plan: Stay awake.* She stared off dreamily and thought of Taylor Jackson Singer.

26

In **her junior** year at American University, in the expensive northwest corner of DC, Shelley first lost herself to love. Spencer was a graduate student in international studies, set to embark on an idealistic career as a diplomat. He was five-foot-seven; she could tuck him under her armpit. He was a bullshit artiste supreme, a skilled joke teller, and a passionate lover. Although from a Waspy Rhode Island family, he handled himself with complete ease with regard to their differences in race and culture. His friends, however, didn't behave as well.

At Spencer's birthday bash, a suburban brat recounted the story of how he'd survived the horror of getting lost while driving through the world's most menacing ghetto. He was describing Shelley's neighborhood.

One felt compelled to discuss with her all he had learned in sociology class about the prejudices Black people held about the different shades of their own race.

Still others peppered her with a variety of political questions as though she were the sole representative from Negro Planet.

A head taller than anyone else, she discovered she was being used as a landmark when directing partygoers to the restroom.

One kid challenged her on whether she was urban enough. "Yes, you're obviously African-American, but you've never been poor."

"What makes you say that?"

"Because you're well-spoken, smart. Not like ..." Already too late, he caught himself and changed direction. "You can afford an expensive school."

"I'm on scholarship."

"Really? What sport?"

Her eyes narrowed. "Academic."

"And you're studying criminal justice? That's like the phys ed of degrees."

Afterwards, she'd had a monumental fight with Spencer over his choice of friends.

"They're really not that bad," he said.

"They're evil! They're a whole new mutant form of evil."

"You've just been under a lot of pressure lately."

He was right. Shelley's father had had an accident ten years back. He was paralyzed from the neck down and in recent months he had begun deteriorating rapidly. She felt torn in pieces between school and Spencer, her home and her father's sickbed. With her father's failing health, her family's finances, shaky in recent years, had tanked. Her scholarship paid her academic expenses—but it wasn't enough. She'd taken to attending random seminars where food was being served. There were times she was too poor to buy a Metro pass so she had to spend two hours on a series of city buses to wend her way home. And Spencer was getting set to graduate and take a post overseas—in Finland.

"Come with me," he'd said. "In Scandinavia you'll be so exotic you'll be worshiped as a goddess."

"I prefer to be worshiped as plain old me."

She pleaded with him to stay. She wasn't ready to leave behind her career goals, her family, her community, her entire world, along with everything she knew and held dear. When he stuck with his plans, she decided she had to let him go.

She composed a break-up note and set it inside a bon voyage card behind the face of the Swedish Chef Muppet.

He pointed out that he was headed to Finland, not Sweden.

She asked him to make their break-up easier and not to write. "It would never work. Diplomats need portable families and I don't fit in a suitcase."

She became really angry when he didn't even try fighting to keep her. And how dare he listen to her and not even send a letter?

27

SOMEWHERE AROUND FOUR A.M., Mira was startled awake by a clattering bang. She wore one of Shelley's pullovers as pajamas, the fringe drooping below her knees. With the shirt sleeves empty and dangling, and arms folded across her chest, she shuffled down the hallway determined to discover what had caused the racket. There she found Shelley hugging Cassidy's corpse. Moments ago, when its knees buckled, it had banged against the shelves, knocking over and spilling gallon jugs of bleach and ammonia. The liquids had emptied over its body. The fumes choked like tear gas.

"The rigor mortis has pretty much played out," Shelley said. "His joints can flex again. It'll be easier to get him in the trunk the next time."

"Okay." Mira turned around and began padding back to bed.

"Hey, girl! It's your turn at patrol. I need some rest. Just keep a look out for anything strange and wake me up if you get worried about anything. The gun is on the recliner."

"And I'll be on the sofa."

"Don't nod off."

"Right, mom."

28

AT SEVEN A.M. Shelley woke to find Mira in the kitchen, clutching a mug of coffee. Her eyes seemed to have withdrawn into her head. She squinted at Shelley. The gun sat atop the kitchen table.

"Anything to report?" Shelley asked.

"I watched some cats fornicate on your lawn. I didn't wake you because it was pretty low-quality porn."

Shelley grabbed a box of cereal and an expired carton of milk. She gave the latter a sniff and decided it was worth the risk. Then she grabbed a mug from the dish rack and headed to her percolator. The now-empty two-quart pot had been three-quarters full when she'd gone to bed.

"This is the game plan," Shelley announced. "I'm going to the hospital to talk to Raffi. Then I'll head to the archives to check out an idea or two. I need you to rustle up that body bag. Once you've got it, come back and guard the house. I'll be back by noon at the latest."

"I'm playing nanny to a dead body again?" Mira asked, incredulous. "Listen, if they wanted to come for us, they would have done it at night. This is *my* game plan: I'm going home to get a change of clothes and grab some Xanax. Then I'll head to the lab to process the piece of rug and your mugful of urine and run the drug analyses. Once I've got all of that done, I'll fetch the body bag. On my way back here, I'll drop by the deli. What do you want for lunch?"

"A gyro. Two."

"Ooh, I could go for one, also. And some salty nibble food." Mira stood up, clutched the back of the chair, and stood for a moment with her eyes shut.

"Are you okay, Mira?"

"No, Shel, I'm not okay. But that's okay."

29

DAYBREAK DID NOTHING to drive the chill from the air; the morning felt ten degrees colder than the night before. The sky was overcast, clouds draped low, one vast smothering dank blanket.

Shelley directed her car's heating vent directly at her face, blasting the sting of weariness from her eyes. A sudden pang of guilt stabbed her conscience. Mira looked up to her, even worshiped her. While this fed Shelley's ego, she recognized she was abusing Mira's trust, placing her at risk. *I'm going to get her killed.*

She would have to send Mira packing. Shelley needed someone with more experience in handling danger. She'd have to drag her partner into this. She phoned Kent.

"Hello." His voice was groggy.

"It's your morning wake-up call."

"I've been on the phone with my girlfriend for the past hour. She woke me up at seven. She doesn't seem to understand the concept of how God made Sundays for sleep-ins ..."

"Your girlfriend?"

"Yeah. Why is sex always so complicated?"

"Because it is." Shelley paused a moment. "By the way, how old is she?"

"Why does that matter?"

"Because you're sleeping with your babysitter."

"Yeah, so what? And who told you?"

"She's still in school. *You* told me that."

Kent chuckled. "Shel, I'm a single father."

"Yeah, you use that line as an answer to everything."

"Think about it, Shel. I've got more than one babysitter. My girlfriend is my divorced neighbor."

Shelley winced. "Shit, Kent. I'm sorry."

"You really thought?"

"Like I said, I'm sorry. Look, Kent, I need your help. I've been working an angle on the investigation, off the radar and a bit dangerous. And illegal."

"You? By-the-book Krieg?"

"I think it's me. Sometimes I'm not sure."

"What do you need?"

Shelley felt instantaneous relief. An officer could always rely on her partner. Closer than marriage, 'til death do us part. "Can you go to the office and find updates on the Hooks case?

Copy whatever you find and meet me at my place in the afternoon, when the assignments will get a bit more dicey."

"I'll have to arrange it with my babysitter. I've been running up a lot of favors."

"Okay, have fun arranging. And thanks, Kent."

30

THE DC CENTRAL Detention Facility operated an adjoining health-care center, medium security. She stowed her weapon with security and received an escort to the elevator.

"Hooks is on the third floor," her chaperone said, pressing the button. "His lawyer left orders to admit no one, especially not the police."

"He'll want to talk with me."

"I doubt that. Because of the civil suit, I'm under instructions. I'll shepherd you in, stay with you until he tells you to go to hell, and then walk you straight out."

The elevator doors parted, revealing a reception room surrounded by thick Plexiglas walls. Shelley signed in with her name and badge number. She flashed her ID at the clerk.

The entry to the hospital floor came at the end of a short tunnel. When the first door opened, they proceeded into a claustrophobic pen. This door shut behind them, an electronic bolt clicking into place. Then the second door opened.

The layout of the recovery ward was much the same as that of any hospital floor, with a semicircular nurses' station adjacent to a long corridor that connected to the recovery rooms. The nurses were beefy and grim. An orderly cracked his knuckles, his hands large enough to crush coconuts. All of the recovery rooms' doors were shut and secured with two locks. At the dead end of the hallway a guard sat on a bolted-down chair studying his iPhone.

Shelley's escort led her to the second door down, then whisked through a ring that held a hundred keys until he found the right ones. When the door opened a woman stood there. She greeted them with a stiff "Hello."

She was a short and bony African-American, nearing fifty, wearing a stylish black dress. She glanced at the guard, then fixed on Shelley's towering figure.

Shelley immediately recognized the family resemblance. "Esmay Hooks," she said. Raffi's mother. The city must be bending over backwards to allow her to visit her son inside a medium-security ward. "I'm ..."

"I know who you are," Esmay said. Her words came out well spaced, each given its own emphasis. "Raffi painted me a fine picture of you."

"I'm sorry about Keshawn."

"Are you?"

Shelley felt a bit sheepish. She had imagined Keshawn and Raffi's mother to be some slobbish, unconcerned welfare mom. Keshawn and Raffi had two different fathers, Keshawn was a drug addict and small-time dealer, Raffi was ... What was Raffi? Not a murderer. A kid getting by. A bullied younger brother. Shelley scolded herself for giving into stereotypes. Esmay looked elegant—and yet Raffi said she didn't have a phone.

"My son is sleeping now," Esmay said. "His dope-drip brings him that relief, at least."

"I believe I can help your son. I'd like to meet with his lawyer, Mrs. Hooks."

"The one defending him or the one suing you?"

"His defense lawyer. I believe I have proof your son is innocent."

"I know my son is innocent. As of now his lawyer is a public defender, Simon Lutz. I expect we'll be upgrading soon. The outrageousness of his beating has brought us offers of free legal service. Perhaps they are publicity hounds. No matter. As long as they are vicious."

"I've been taken off the case. The officers who've replaced me won't help your son. Let me meet with his lawyer and I'll turn over enough evidence to end this." She handed Esmay Hooks her personal card with her cell-phone number.

Esmay squinted at the card. "I'll pass this along."

"Mrs. Hooks? Please don't let them transfer him back to jail, not even juvie. It's not safe. Tell him to fake the extent of his injuries, if necessary."

Shelley looked at the guard by her side. He appeared wide-eyed with amazement at the direction the conversation had taken.

"He won't need any faking," Esmay said. Her expression softened; she searched Shelley's face. "What's in this for you?"

"Just trying to right a wrong."

"We're not dropping the lawsuit."

"I'm not asking you to."

"You can go now," Esmay said. She began to slowly close the door.

As the guard escorted Shelley back to the entrance, he said, "You know, I can see how you must be running this behind command's back. Apologizing when there's a lawsuit? Telling her you can prove her son's innocence? You could get in a shit-load of trouble for what you just did." He chuckled nervously. "It's my job to write this up. But I don't think I will."

31

OVER THE YEARS, Shelley had picked up a trick or two on how to subvert the system. With regard to the DC bureaucracy this didn't mean simply snipping red tape; it meant hacking her way through a jungle with a machete.

When she needed to reach a hard-to-contact government official, instead of ringing his phone line she would increase the number of his extension by one. This usually rang the phone of someone else in the office. A reticent bureaucrat who loathed answering his own line often took calls transferred from a near-by desk.

Another of her schemes would serve her now. She arrived at Central Archives at the perfect day and hour. Only the most inexperienced staff worked Sunday mornings—a lack of seniority meant filling the least-desired shifts. Often young and susceptible to the coercion of authority, always unfamiliar with the minutiae of regulations, such unsuspecting novices could be manipulated to aid Shelley's investigation.

The kid behind the clerk's desk looked eighteen but more than likely he had just graduated college. *Young people are getting younger*, Shelley thought. He kept a half dozen pens in his vest pocket. He gave her a horsey grin, his full set of front upper teeth on display.

"Morning," Shelley began, pleasantly. "I need the log sheets for everyone who checked out C.I. files during the past month."

The kid looked at her quizzically. "I don't think I'm supposed to do that."

Shelley feigned disapproval. "A detective is making a request and you don't even know your own procedures?"

"I could check with my supervisor."

"Or you could follow the basic rules and allow me access to the logs under your supervision."

The clerk stiffened, immobilized by the decision he had to make.

"Now would be good," Shelley said.

That was enough to jolt him into action. He brought back two thick ring binders, filled with sheets of punched paper.

"Thank you," Shelley said. "I should be done in just a few minutes."

SHELLEY HAD IN mind a strategy for locating the other two names on the hit list. First she would determine who had requested Cassidy's C.I. jacket and then flag the other folders that officer had checked out. With this information she could then requisition those files to determine whether they had also disappeared. If one or more officers could be matched to all the missing files, she might learn the identity or identities of her enemies.

She encountered Cassidy's name soon enough. On the same day, the petitioner solicited the C.I. files for both Cassidy Higgins and Keshawn Davies. *So Davies did have a snitch jacket*, Shelley thought. The detective making both requests: Lieutenant Kris Atchison.

She flipped through the pages, making notes about all of Atch's requests. By the time she was done, she had a list of eight names. She jotted down all of Morretti's petitions, too. He had checked out the same file over and over again: Sheena Vance.

When Shelley finished, she returned the logs to the clerk.

"Just one more thing, please," she said. "I'm going to request several files, but all you have to do is inform me whether they exist."

"If they are in the log book, they exist."

"We'll see." She handed over her list.

"You'll need to fill out a request slip for each," the clerk said.

"No. That's only if I need you to bring me the files." Someday he would learn the correct procedures. But not today.

"All right," he said. He went to his computer station and began to type in names. On a sheet of scratch paper he wrote down the locations of the files.

"Five of these names don't even have computer records," he said. "That's not supposed to happen. Still, they should be in place alphabetically."

He disappeared into the back rooms. After about twenty minutes he returned and handed back her slip of paper. "The checkmarks are the absent files, the same as those without computer entries. I guess they got misplaced or something."

Among those missing were Cassidy Higgins and Keshawn Davies. Those names she already knew. However, she could add three more to her list: Sheena Vance, Billy Olsen, and Alfred Zahn. *Alfred Zahn*. AZ.

She thanked the clerk. As she was about to leave she noticed that one of the pens he kept in his vest protector was a yellow fluorescent highlighter.

"Can I borrow your yellow marker for a second?" she asked.

The clerk reflexively guarded his vest pocket. Then he carefully extracted and offered her the highlighter.

She popped its cap and pinched her fingers near its felt nib. She crushed the tip, trying to simulate the anguish Keshawn must have felt when he was being tortured and forced to write names. "Could you hand me your legal pad?"

He placed it on the counter. Shelley mushed the pen's tip against the pad and spelled out the names Alfred Zahn, Sheena Vance, and Billy Olsen.

The first flaw in her experiment came when the ink of the yellow highlighter disappeared into the yellow paper of the pad. She checked the page underneath for bleed-through. Although the ink was invisible, she could feel some moistness beneath her fingertips. She examined her thumb and index fingers. They were stained with a fluorescent yellow oval.

A revelation struck her. She returned the pad and pen to the clerk.

"Thank you," she said. "You've been very helpful." She needed to get back to her house and examine the crime-scene photos again.

32

"KENT?" SHELLEY SPOKE on her cellular while negotiating one of Washington's treacherous traffic circles. Even with the sparseness of vehicles that came with Sunday noon, navigating these felt like spinning the cylinder of a revolver in a game of Russian Roulette.

"Shel. It's been freaky at the office. Click and Atch are eyeing me like I'm some kind of spy, which I guess I am. They won't let me touch the files and I'd swear the folder is growing thinner, not fatter. You know that spooky smile Click makes when he pretends that a breeze just happened to blow him by your desk? Well, that wind has been blowing here every five minutes. They suspect I'm up to something and they keep asking about you."

"Hang in there. I need you to run some names for me. DMV, NCIC, NADDIS, the works. I'm guessing any Metro criminal records will have disappeared. I'll take whatever you can find, but especially addresses, contacts, and aliases. The names are Sheena Vance, Billy Olsen with an 'e,' and Alfred Zahn, Z-A-H-N."

"AZ?"

"Yeah."

"I can tell you up front, no one's got a handle on him. He's never been processed."

Shelley thought about the AZ legend. Cops said he maintained a peculiar set of ethics. As a dealer, he trafficked solely in smack, deeming crack and meth too destructive. He bought and moved into abandoned houses. Then, like any other drug-slinger, he set up an impenetrable fortress from which he conducted his trade. While shut up in the house he renovated it and, before he could be pinpointed and raided, he transferred the ownership to a local charity. Once, when the police tried seizing one of his former properties under drug-forfeiture laws, community organizations and local politicians fought back. Depending on whom you spoke to, AZ was either an opportunist bribing neighbors and politicos to look the other way or a ghetto hero.

"Any notion on how to find him?" she asked.

"First District, Shaw and north, give or take a mile. If we could nail down where he's operating we would have busted him long ago."

Kent dropped his voice to just above a hush. "This case has stirred up yet another shitstorm. Some woman busted into Raffi's place, the crime scene, last night. She didn't even bother to close the door on the way out. One of the neighbors called it in. Saw a short female leaving the scene—so I guess you're in the clear. The witness got a plate number but must have read it wrong. A Virginia tag but one digit short of reality."

Oh, shit, Shelley thought. *I still have the boat's license plate on my car.*

"And we've piqued the curiosity of the FBI," Kent went on. "I caught the call from their central office, an Agent Ansel Ballinger, Ballin-juh as he says it. He got word of Ernesto Grey's rib injuries and seemed interested in the MO. He left a contact number." Kent recited it twice.

Shelley jotted it down. "Got it."

"With DC and Maryland involved, this case cuts across jurisdictions," Kent continued. "The feds may be getting ready to swoop down on us."

"What did you tell Ballinger?"

"I didn't volunteer anything. He only knows about Grey. I kept mum on how Raffi had the same sort of mutilation. I also didn't tell Atch or Click about the call. Speaking of which ... got to go. My new best amigo is oozing over for a schmooze. I'll see you at your place later."

33

MIRA SAT PERCHED on the step up to the front door of Shelley's house, a folded body bag across her lap. She wore a black skin-tight jumpsuit with long sleeves and a ski cap, clothing suited for cat-burgling. With her arms crossing her chest and her hands clasping her shoulders, she hugged herself tightly as though bundled in a straitjacket, shivering and rocking to keep herself warm. Next to her feet a white sack bled with translucent patches of grease. Gyros.

Upon Shelley's arrival in the driveway, Mira bounced to her feet.

The garage door lumbered open. Mira followed the Malibu inside. "I just got here," she said.

"We have a lot to talk about." Taking a small screwdriver from her handbag, Shelley knelt down behind her license plates and proceeded to remove the boat tag.

"Okay," Mira said. "I'll go first. Both the rug and your pee showed residues of GHB. Now GHB could have been used to knock you and Raffi out, but usually it takes a while to work, and you'd feel woozy before you passed out. I came across another suspicious metabolite that I couldn't identify because I've never run across it before. It's a compact molecule, low molecular weight with tight bonding, the kind that can be absorbed easily and then gets sopped up straight into the brain like an IV anesthetic. You'd be out like a light. This type of drug can pass through the skin with a pat on the shoulder or a handshake. So, I'm thinking they slimed you and Raffi with the knockout drug and then they injected the two of you with GHB to wipe clean your memories."

"Did you bring a copy of the lab results?"

"Chromatograms and all. They're in my purse."

"We'll pass them along to Raffi's lawyer."

"And I brought a body bag from the funeral parlor. It's not like the kind they use for crime scenes, it doesn't come with handles. It's just a seven-foot vinyl sack with a zipper. I was told it's crematorium safe, whatever that means."

Having removed the boat license plate, Shelley brushed past Mira. She unlocked the house door and stepped inside to suspend the alarm.

Mira cruised into the kitchen ahead of Shelley. She made a quick pivot and, with a snap of her wrists, unfurled the body bag.

Shelley scooted into a kitchen chair and planted her elbows on top of the table. "Mira, have a seat, please."

"Is this going to be one of your den-mother talks?"

"Mira, this is already a risky operation and it's bound to get even more dangerous. I've already asked too much of you. You should go home."

"But you need my help. Don't worry, I can deal with this."

"No, you can't," Shelley said. "You think you can, but it isn't just about the mind-fuck of dragging around a corpse and staring at bloody photos. Some bad people have targeted me. I don't want you in their crosshairs."

"When did you decide this? And who gave you permission to choose for me?"

"This isn't a game. I don't want you to get hurt. You prance in here like some teen dressed for a Goth party."

"Goth? Girl, do you even know what Goth looks like? These clothes are maybe a little Emo or Old Navy hipster, or just, I don't know, practical for sneaking around in the dark. Jesus, Shel, why do I even like you? You're such a Joe Friday. Do you know what the most fundamental principle of being human is? It goes like this. It's my life, nobody else's. So I get to live it."

"Mira, I don't want you dead."

"Thank you. The feeling is mutual. Now, let's get to work."

Shelley shrugged with tense resignation. She should have predicted Mira wouldn't take orders quite so easily.

As a peace offering, Shelley raised a palm, then twisted her wrist to display the yellow stain on the pinching surface of her thumb and index finger. "I played around with a marker."

"What's with that yellow?"

Shelley shuffled through the crime-scene photos on her kitchen table. "Keshawn's fingers had a purple smudge where he squeezed the pen." She flopped the photo in front of Mira. "The yellow pad he wrote on, however, had green blotches. This means the felt pen tip was thick and mushy and ... blue. Blue when it mixed with the red of blood turned purple. When it smudged into the yellow pad ..."

" ... it became green," Mira said. She studied the photocopies. "Lookie here." Along with the color copies the put-upon secretary had made a simple black and white of each. "In the color photos, around the purple blotches on his fingers there's a halo of light blue. But that disappears in the black and white. It's a type of ink called non-photo blue. Layout editors use it to mark up documents so they can insert notes that won't show up when the document gets copied or printed."

"A layout editor? Like for newspapers and magazines?"

"Others use it, too. Pen and ink artists. I've seen an ME use it to scribble down notes, a rough draft before deciding what she wanted to keep."

Shelley nodded, taking this in. "While at the archives I came up with three names: Alfred Zahn, Billy Olsen, and Sheena Vance. Alfred Zahn goes by the name AZ. He's a legend on the streets. He keeps a mysterious hideaway like Ali Baba and his den of thieves. Tough to track down. I have Kent searching for info on the other two."

Shelley set the photocopy of the yellow pad in front of her. Three lines of green dots, bleedthrough, represented the names the killers had forced Keshawn to write. She had already filled in Cassidy's name. While scanning the page, only now did she realize how short the second line was, dots forming a triangle and a zigzag. AZ. She wrote in the initials connecting the blotches. The third line of dots stretched out to the normal length of a name. Billy Olsen fit perfectly. Sheena Vance, however, was not part of the list.

Shelley stared at the names. Her moment of triumph in spelling out the list quickly passed and now she felt oddly defeated. Even with the names identified, she still felt clueless as to what was going on or why.

"I have a feeling Billy Olsen may be the next hit," Shelley said. "AZ will be hard to locate—for us or for an assassin."

"And Vance?"

"She was Click's C.I. The other two come from Atch."

"Then it's Atch we have to worry about? I was really hoping it would be that asshole, Click."

"You've never even met him, Mira."

"So, what's your point?"

"He's much more fun to hate after you get to know him." Shelley half-smiled. "Click could be involved. Click and Atch along with the Maryland detectives, not to mention that blond guy with a gun. We really don't know how many or where this ends. Kent will be here soon. Maybe he'll give us some idea of who these people are on the hit list."

"Good. Now, let's bag that body. I mean Cassidy. Your friend."

34

WITH THE RIGOR mortis slackening, the cocooned corpse had toppled out of the garbage container and crumpled against the closet wall. Its waist bowed and its knees buckled as it settled down. Its head lolled to the side. Its tongue, gray and swollen, protruded from its mouth and pressed against the cellophane. Maggots carpeted the closet floor.

"I hope these mortuary bags lock in the smell," Mira said.

"When we're done I'll fire up an incense candle."

They spread out the bag along the hall floor. Shelley tugged the plastic zipper around the D-shaped flap and flipped open the covering. Then she grabbed Cassidy under his chin and hauled him to his feet. She dragged him backwards until his rear end sat in the middle of the bag's inside space. She laid his shoulders and head down and stretched out his legs. Once all was in place, she tugged the bag's sides up and slid the zipper along its long track, sealing him inside.

"This is better," Mira said. "This is respectful. He's where he should be." For a few moments neither said a word, both staring at the full body bag lying in the hallway.

"Get the Dust Buster and suck up some maggots," Shelley said. "I'll carry the garbage can to the shower for a good rinsing."

35

THEY ATE LUNCH in relative silence. Shelley's stomach already felt like a gurgling kettle of acid, and the spicy gyros only added to the caustic brew. Back in her early days on the force, when each shift assaulted her senses, numbed her mind, and fired up a severe case of heartburn, she used to keep a bottle of Gaviscon in her fridge. She wished she had some now.

"Kent should be here any minute," Shelley said. "If he's not here in a few, I'll call."

"Are we going to introduce him to our friend in the hallway?"

"No. That would risk his career and, as he regularly informs me, he's a single father."

Shelley thought for a moment. "I busted this one drug dealer," she said, "who kept a storage space above his garage door. He rigged it so the only way you could turn on the garage light was by opening the garage door. When the door did open, its panels hid his stash. When it closed, the light cut off, and you couldn't see the space."

"But couldn't you just point a flashlight?" Mira asked.

"That was the trick. When I visited the garage, I didn't think I needed one. The open door brought all the illumination I needed: sunlight and the bank of fluorescents overhead. I've got the same sort of gap above my door. I'll add a couple of planks to hold Cassidy and rewire the light switch to the garage-door motor."

"You'd make a great criminal, Shel."

"This *is* criminal, Mira. I *am* a great criminal. And let me tell you, it's unnerving."

Shelley chose not to dwell on it, instead picking up her phone and punching in the number of the FBI agent.

"Ballinjuh."

"This is Detective Shelley Krieg, Metro PD."

"DC Metro?"

"Is there any other?"

Ballinger responded with silence.

"You called us asking about the Ernesto Grey case?"

"That's right. Routine follow-up on account of what I got running this search aggregator for terms with this murder's peculiarities. It coughed up a report from an NCIC check on a case in Maryland regarding a rib-choppuh. I called a Mt. Rainier captain who said his guy was out but I oughta check in with you." Ballinger had a tamped-down New England drawl,

Shelley noted. He lost his R's only when they came at the end of sentences.

"Can you tell me why you're looking for this particular MO?"

"I'll swap stories with you if you got something for me."

His tone was so casual she imagined him leaning back in his chair, relaxed and completely uninterested in what some local yokel had to say.

"How's this? There's been a second case."

She heard a clunking sound as though the chair's front legs had just hit the floor.

"Okay, ma'am. You got my ears prickling."

"That's where Metro PD comes in. Another African-American male killed in an identical manner. This one had his fingers cut off."

"But not his thumb?" Ballinger asked.

Bingo-bingo-bingo, Shelley thought, all the alarms in her mind ringing at once. "No, not his thumb."

"Do either of your cases have connections to Russia? Russian suspects, Russian mob?"

"Before I answer that, I could use some help with my investigation."

"I'm not at liberty to discuss these mattuhs."

"Can I tell you something off the record?"

"How far removed from the recuhd?"

"There's another bit of intel, but I acquired it during an illegal act."

"How remote from legal?"

"If I were caught, I suspect they'd slap me with a suspension but not a jail sentence. I got a bit creative in my police work."

"I'm a true-blue fan of creativity." His tone had turned somewhat flirtatious. "Your secret stays private with me."

"Last night I made a rogue visit to the crime scene to get a second look. While there, I found someone else hanging around. Josef Serov."

It was a guess, but Ballinger's response confirmed she had hit the target: He whistled. His accent, previously held in check, went full-Boston. "Ah you frickin' with me? Cause if you'da seen him, you'da sure not be breathing to tell about it."

She described her encounter.

When she finished, silence. Finally, Ballinger spoke. "Sounds like my guy. I've been on his tail now for a lifetime. But nobody knows if Serov is his true name or just an alias. Along with mob enforcer, he's hired out as a mercenary assassin, mostly in the Balkans and along the Aegean rim. He travels with a translator. Seems he's never been handy at picking up languages. No sign he's come stateside before, but he still holds onto a spot near the top of our watch list.

"Be careful, Krieg. He's a merciless bastuhd. He even spooks the Dark Art folks over at the Agency. Still—okay, let me speak frankly. I'm not exactly buying you saw him—the Loch Ness monster makes more public appearances. But, whether it was a genuine sighting or not, it's worth some follow-up. I'll be sending a be-on-the-lookout to the Secret Service and I'll get our task force to pay you a business call."

"Third District," Shelley said. "And, if I'm not in, talk to Lieutenants Morretti and Atchison. They're the leads on this case."

"As hit men go, Serov's at the top of the food chain. He comes with a hellacious price tag. Exactly what kind of investigation are you working, Detective Krieg?"

"The murder of a pair of low-level dealers."

"Not possible. You may be thinking that you're tweaking on navel fuzz but you're yanking at the whiskers of a ten-foot tiguh. You got hold of a whole nuther beast. And Detective Krieg, don't go pursuing Serov on your lonesome. When it's not futile, it's fatal. Going after him is like chasing a vampire in a mirror maze. He shows no reflection and he's got no shadow. When you think you trapped him in a corner you'll find he's tap-tapping the back of your shoulder. Two years ago, in Athens, Interpol had him corralled in a hotel room surrounded by a strike force. He killed three of their officers and evaporated. Poof. Detective Krieg? Shelley? Stay put on this until we meet up. If it's Serov, then let's fuck that bugger togethuh."

"Looking forward to it."

"I'll text you my email address so you can pass along any relevant files." His voice dropped. She heard a squeak-squeak as he swiveled back and forth in his chair. "Umm ... let me guess—you're a slinky blonde with a husky voice."

"Nailed it. Five-foot-two with heaving bosoms. Are you hitting on me?"

"Oh, lady, I'm trying. I'm trying."

SHELLEY TOLD MIRA the details of her talk with Ballinger, trying once again to scare her friend off of the case.

"We're in this to the end, Shel. Like Thelma and Louise."

"Great image. Headed straight off a cliff."

While Mira prepared an official lab report to turn over to Raffi's lawyer, Shelley built a hiding place for Cassidy in the garage. The rewiring was simple. She had learned basic circuits in a shop class she'd taken in high school.

With supporting planks set in place atop the ceiling's cross-beams, Shelley dragged the body bag into her garage and, with the aid of a ladder, heaved it up to stow it in the space above her garage door. The bag sealed in most of the odors. Only when she raised the bundle overhead did she get a whiff of its contents.

She tested her work by pressing the button on the remote to roll open the garage door. The hinges of its pleated panels crimped as it drew back and up, concealing her stash and revealing Kent standing hand in hand with his five-year-old daughter, Kimmy.

36

Kent's free hand held several manila folders.

"Hey there," Kent said.

"Hi, Miss Shelley," Kimmy said.

"Hi, sweetie." Shelley dropped down on one knee and wrapped the child in an embrace.

Kimmy broke free. "You smell like yuck."

"I've been doing some housework."

"You smell like a tree fart," the child said.

Her father pinched his daughter's shoulder gently. "That's enough, Kimmy."

Kimmy broke free, scampering over to the ladder, which she started climbing.

Kent spoke in a hush. "When Kimmy and I were in the woods for a hike, I came across a deer carcass. I kept her from seeing it but she asked, 'What's that smell?' So I told her it was a tree fart."

Shelley wrenched Kimmy off the ladder's top rungs, gave her a turn, and clasped the child to her chest. The kid fought her captivity with all her might.

Mira peeked into the garage.

"Kent, Kimmy, this is my friend Yasmira Tamer," Shelley said.

"Call me Mira."

Kimmy slipped free and rushed Mira, attacking her leg with a pro-wrestling hold.

"You smell like a fart sandwich," the child said.

"What a *delightful* little girl," Mira said, ripping herself from the child's grip.

Kimmy tried maneuvering past Mira, who snatched the child by her belt.

"Shel, could you cover up some of the icky photos on the table?" Mira asked.

As Kimmy's feet pedaled in place, Shelley and Kent entered the kitchen and swept the crime-scene photos into a folder.

"Really, Kent. It's Bring Your Child to Work Day?"

"This is who I am, Shelley."

"You couldn't arrange ...?"

"No."

"Okay, Kimmy," Mira said as she and Kimmy joined Shelley and Kent at the table. "Let's find you something good on television."

"No, thanks." Kimmy plopped down in a chair in front of the table, one of the team. "There are worms in your scoop."

Shelley had to think twice to interpret this statement. The Dust Buster on her counter had the shape of a sandbox shovel. Maggots wriggled from its mouth.

Kent shot Shelley a fiery glare.

Mira herded Kimmy down the hallway, saying, "Let's find something to do."

With a poke of his index finger Kent smashed a maggot. "What the hell are you up to, Shel?"

"Just enough to make my head explode. Kent, Mira works in the crime lab. She ran a section of hall carpet with Raffi's urine and found GHB, the date-rape drug. It causes amnesia."

"That could be all that's needed to kill the case against him." Kent thought for a moment. "Wait a sec. The part of the rug where Raffi sat wasn't taken into evidence. *You* were the one who trespassed on the crime scene."

"I had to. Listen, Kent. I knew Raffi was innocent because the same thing happened to me. Late Friday night someone, I don't know who, came here and drugged me the same way."

Shelley allowed a moment for this information to sink in.

"The maggots ... What? They left a horse's head in your bed?"

"Something like that."

"Then what?"

"Don't ask, you don't want to know."

"But I *am* asking."

"And I'm telling you, you don't want to know."

"You called me in. I'm your partner."

"And you brought a five-year-old. That tells me you should stay out of this."

"You're tying your own noose. And if you shut me out, Shel, I won't be around to stop you from hanging yourself."

"Glad to know you're concerned."

Kent pinched his forehead. "Okay, I'll find someone to watch Kimmy. I'll be there for you. But you've got to fill me in. You've got to show me at least that much respect."

Shelley decided she couldn't risk telling him the truth, so she compromised by choosing a respectful lie. "Friday night, someone broke into my house and left behind a dead dog, ribs cut open. They visited again last night. And they left a reminder."

"A reminder?"

"A warning to stay off this case."

"Jesus, Shel. That's scary. Maybe Raffi has a gang."

"It's not about Raffi. It's more than that."

"Okay. It doesn't matter. Someone broke into your house. You've got to bring this to Tate."

"I don't know, Kent. I don't trust the department."

"Why not?"

"I have reasons. I'm almost certain Atch and Click are involved. And the Maryland detectives? Do you really believe a bloody fingerprint showed up on a watch and no one noticed it until now?"

"Fingerprints are hard to fake, Shel."

"Not if it comes from Keshawn's missing finger."

"Oh, jeez. I saw the print. It was pinkie-sized ..."

"Left pinkie?"

"I don't know. If that's what it is then ... shit." Kent exhaled. "I agree Atch and Click are acting suspicious. But Tate assigned this case to you and me even after those two were first on the scene."

"And he took the case away from me. Besides, even if Tate is clean, is he going to run the investigation himself? Who's he going to bring in on it? I can't trust anyone, not until I have a better idea of what's going on."

"That's paranoid."

"Not knowing who to trust? Yeah, it's making me a bit neurotic."

Kent nodded grimly. "Okay. I surrender. I'll be back here tonight. Without Kimmy. You said they visited Friday and Saturday night? So they'll be waiting for dark."

He sighed, again pinching his forehead. Then he slapped three portfolios on the table. "The three you asked about." He opened the first folder, a single sheet. "Alfred Zahn, AZ, has a box-sized file filled with useless information. No photo and no current whereabouts. I compiled a list of some of his likely associates."

The second folder. "Billy Olsen, AKA Crank. He's done time for possession—twice. On top of that, he once got cited for vagrancy and panhandling and was hauled in by the Capitol Police for begging on the mall. His arrest reports describe him as homeless, NFA. Family in Seattle, their numbers are included if you want to make a call. Best guess—they haven't spoken in years. Nothing in his write-ups to pin a residence on him—except for this—a parking meter cop wrote him a citation for jaywalking a month ago."

"Someone wrote a homeless man a jaywalking ticket?"

"On the ticket it says he threw a can of peaches at a meter scooter and missed. I suspect the officer got pissed off and played street court, whacking him with jaywalking, the worst pedestrian offense she could write up. It lists his residence as 2100 Evarts, Northeast, the old AME shelter."

The thumb-sized photo of Olsen showed him with wild hair stabbing out in every direction, stiffened by the muck of months without a shower. His face seemed sunburnt and scabby, the bridge of his nose broken and flattened. Even his gaze appeared beaten as though the blows of a lost life had channeled directly into his eye sockets.

Kent opened the third folder, which contained a single slip of paper with scratched-out notes. "No one by the name of Sheena Vance has a criminal history, not even a parking ticket. DMV lists two women with that name living in the District: one is sixty-five, the other twenty-five. One number showed up in the phone book. I tried ringing. The twenty-five-year-old. Her answering machine message was ... let's say, suggestive. Um ... professional." His cheeks reddened.

"She was on Click's list." Shelley squinted, making the connection. "Kent, what do you know about snitch-snatch?"

"Snitch-snatch? I've caught rumors of it, sort of a departmental legend." He perked up his ears, listening for Kimmy. The silence told him it was safe for him to proceed. "An officer digs up a lead to solve a case or make a raid. He invents the claim that the lead came from a certain working girl who acted as his confidential informant. He fills out the forms and gets money from the C.I. funds to pay the girl. She signs off as a phony informant and he gets laid."

"I've never heard ..."

"It's just locker-room swagger. Guys mouthing off."

"I overheard Click say, 'We'll have to hold back on the snitch-snatch.'"

"Hmm. Okay. But I don't see how that fits in with the rest."

"Neither do I."

"Though if I suspected *anyone* of getting some snitch-snatch, it would be Click. I ..." Kent cut his sentence short as Kimmy ran in and leapt onto his lap. "I've got some arranging to do," he told Shelley. "I'll see you tonight."

Shelley nodded. "Kent, thanks for everything. The stress is ..."

He clasped his hands around hers. "Take care of yourself, kiddo."

37

MIRA REVERSED A chair and straddled it, spreading her legs around the base of its ladder-back. "What now, *ke-mo sah-bee?*"

"How you holding up?"

"Much better now that I'm medicated."

"You have to be careful. Xanax can own your ass."

"It's legal. I have a prescription—or two."

Shelley decided to drop the subject. "If you say so. Kent gave me some background on the three names. I got a phone number for Vance but I'll need to track down Olsen and AZ. Olsen is homeless and a scrounger. There's a good chance he'll be out begging until night drives him indoors. I've got one location to look for him. If he's not there, we'll scour the city shelters. AZ is an odd sort of chivalrous drug trafficker, a nomad, setting up shop at one dope house before hopping to the next. I have no idea how to begin to find him, but then my head is more full of fog than clear thinking. I tried adding up the number of hours I've slept in the past two nights and I couldn't count straight. I'm going to take a nap but first, I'm going to take a shower. I smell like tree farts."

"Shower and bed. Mind if I join you?"

"Mira ..."

"Jeez, Shel, you are so easy to get got. Just like when we first met."

"Mira, if you wouldn't mind ... Here's the number for a Sheena Vance." She handed over a sheet of paper. "Kent says she's probably a professional. We need her address and a time for a meet-up. Tell her Lieutenant Sal Morretti referred you and you're looking for some snitch-snatch."

AFTER A LONG, hot shower, Shelley crawled naked under her blankets. Her skin felt rubbery, hydrated, and still tingling. The moment her eyes shut, she heard a doorbell. *Leave me alone.* When she lifted her lids she discovered it was night. No, not night, just the reflux of a memory. It was Saturday before dawn and her clock read 3:36. Her heating vent hummed. In the kitchen her refrigerator motor rumbled. The doorbell sounded again.

The electricity is still on, Shelley thought. *They haven't invaded the house yet.*

She got up, slipped into her sweatpants. Her present voice told her, *don't answer it*, but she had no choice. The memory drew her into her living room. She couldn't turn her head to see from side to side. Invisible cords pulled her, her feet not touching the floor, her body gliding toward the front door. She peered through the peephole, her eye met by a blinding light.

"Who is it?" she asked.

"Who is it?" she repeated, but now she lay on her bed and it was Sunday afternoon again. A sharp pain kicked her belly. Her throat tasted of acid. Her sheets were soaked with sweat.

Shelley tensed her brow, squeezed her eyes closed, and attempted to force the vision to replay, desperate to learn its ending. It didn't return.

Soon she fell asleep. This time she dreamt of showering. She was joined by Taylor Jackson Singer.

38

WHEN SHELLEY NEXT awoke, her clock read 2:32. *Back to real time*, she thought. The sky outside appeared so grim and gray that she struggled for a moment to grasp whether it was day or night, finally realizing she'd slept only an hour and a half. She swung her legs over the side of the bed and paused a moment to allow her blood to locate her brain.

She got up and got dressed, pulling a warm wool sweater over her head. She wedged her feet into her running shoes. Although sometimes she wore high heels to appear even taller, she suspected today's challenges would require fleetness of foot.

When she tramped into the kitchen she found Mira studying the crime-scene photos. Her friend had sketched a crude diagram of Raffi's apartment with stick figures representing Raffi, Keshawn, and the killers.

"Shel, look at this." Shelley moved behind Mira, leaning over the photo spread.

"They sat Keshawn at the table while they snipped off his fingers," Mira said. "There wasn't that much blood on the table because one of them was holding his arm to the side. Look at how the fountains of blood spray all come from this point."

"Keeping him restrained required some heavy-duty force."

"I'm figuring two torturers. One to hold his arm to the side, one to clip off the fingers. There's a way of twisting a thumb that can be very painful and can force compliance. I'm guessing that's why they saved the thumb for last."

From the way Mira discussed such macabre details so matter-of-factly, Shelley thought, she seemed like a desensitized homicide veteran.

"Makes sense," Shelley said.

Mira continued. "What's more, they didn't cuff his wrists because they needed him to have one free hand to do the writing and the other ... well, the other they were mutilating. So, to keep him in place, they must have tied down his feet. But there weren't any binding marks on his legs or ankles. So I looked a bit further." She held up a photo of Keshawn's shoes. "Brand new Nikes laced up to the second-to-last row. The top rows of metal eyeholes in both shoes are torn out. They tied his laces to the chair legs. Then he struggled so hard he started to tear apart his shoes. When they were done torturing him, they untied him, pulling the laces out."

Shelley stared at the photo. "No, not his laces," she said. "His legs would have been jerking with such force against the bindings that the knots would have cinched tight and become a bear to untie, so they would have just cut them. They didn't. Still, the torn eyelets are a good find. I'm guessing they threaded Plasticuffs through the eyelets."

"Plasticuffs? So you're figuring the cops did more than just contaminate the investigation, they directed the actual killing?"

"This I know for sure. For Cassidy's murder, in my bedroom, the only people I would have let in at three or four in the morning would be family or a cop."

Mira fingered through her notes. She found a scribbled number, which she passed to Shelley. "You got a call from Raffi's lawyer. He's free to meet and wants to hook up soon. He seems anxious to hear you out. Whatever you told Raffi's mother, you caught their interest."

"We'll make him first on the agenda," Shelley said. She took her phone from her pocket.

"And, um ... one more thing. I connected with Sheena Vance."

"The one who got Kent to blush."

"Ooh baby! Her voice. Okay, it's gotta be some sort of act, but still ... she purrs when she talks. She sounds like a real pro. If you're not up to it, I could handle the interview alone."

"In your dreams." Shelley opened her cellular. "I'll call the lawyer, then we'll hit the road."

"I'm playing chauffeur again?"

"My getaway driver."

"Okay. That's a tad more cool. Plays better on my résumé." Mira rose and stretched. "Give me a minute. I need a shower. I smell like a fart sandwich."

"Mm-hmm," Shelley responded, concentrating on dialing the phone. She pressed the receiver to her ear. Two rings.

"Hello?"

39

SHELLEY STARED OUT of the passenger's window. The overcast sky was a forbidding gray. A miserable chill had seeped in from the north. The weatherman spoke of sleet arriving come nightfall, a January storm in October. She already had enough gloom on her plate. She switched off the car radio.

Mira upped the heater to full blast. "Where's global warming when you need it? This Catwoman outfit works fine for sneaking around. Now, it's only good for freezing my ass off."

"I've been racking my brain about the victims, asking myself who would pay an expensive hit man to kill petty criminals. But, let's face it, how could Click and Atch be involved in some international plot? They're the Abbott and Costello of law enforcement. None of this makes sense."

"Maybe the guy you saw wasn't Serov."

"It's his MO. Ballinger mentioned leaving the thumb be-hind. Ballinger tried to play it down, but he was excited by the connections."

"All right, then. We have to think bigger. What would bring a mob hit man from Russia to DC?"

"Assassination?" Shelley asked and then immediately shook off her own suggestion. "No assassin would announce his pres-ence by murdering and mutilating low-level street snitches."

"Money?" Mira suggested. "You said that Ernesto was snitching against drug dealers. Maybe he found out something about a major deal."

"And then Serov mutilated the bodies to send a message. It's possible—I can buy that."

"Okay, so Ernesto, Keshawn, Cassidy, and those other guys stumbled onto a big score, burning the Russian mob, which then called in their enforcer."

Shelley's mind rejected Mira's theory. She had to figure out why. All she said was, "No."

"No?"

"No way. I knew Cassidy. He was hardly a high-rolling criminal. Billy Olsen was arrested for tossing canned fruit at a scooter. And Ernesto and Keshawn? Not one of them seemed to have struck a jackpot. They were small-time hustlers who were still hunting down pocket change."

"Which leaves the police," Mira said.

"Which leaves the police," Shelley echoed. She became quiet, focusing her thoughts. Then she said, "A huge wad of drug money was stolen from the Russian mob. By the police.

The mob called in their top enforcer. The police planted evidence to pin the crime on some of their informants."

"I think that covers most of what we know," Mira said.

Shelley shook her head. "Only it doesn't work. Planting evidence, making sure that evidence got under the noses of the mob, and having it point exactly to one group of people and not making it look too convenient? I don't think so. Someone with the police must be working with the mob. They trust him. He's been leading them by the hand. So, let's try this: While working for the mob, Usher learned about a stash of money that he and his dirty cops went on to boost. Usher led the mob on the hunt for the money. He pinned the crime on Ernesto Grey, someone who had already ratted out some drug busts. Usher invited Grey to their regular meeting place. Usher showed up early; he couldn't allow Ernesto to talk or be captured by the mob because they would figure out he's a dupe. Once there, Usher rigged an overdose to kill Ernesto before Serov arrived."

"How do you do that?"

"With a junkie, it's easy. Usher handed over a freebie, not telling him it was ten times more concentrated. Or maybe he laced it with strychnine. Ernesto thought he'd hit the jackpot, so he shot up. When Serov appeared, his target was knocked out, near death. So he performed his calling-card surgery as a message to others who would fuck with the mob."

"If the snitches had nothing to do with the crime, then why did they torture Keshawn for hours to get names? If there was no conspiracy, it would be clear he had no names to give. And why did Keshawn write down the names of more snitches?"

Shelley had no answer. Instead she added to the questions. "And what about AZ? He's no ordinary dealer and not your average snitch."

They pulled up in front of the Moultrie Courthouse.

40

ITS LIMESTONE FACADE rising eight stories, the Moultrie Courthouse at Judiciary Square was a daunting structure: an overgrown bunker, a modernist fortress. Its entrance stood away from the street, across a broad cement courtyard guarded by squat bronze pillars sunk into the concrete, placed there to halt the approach of terrorist vehicles and car bombs. Inside, its lobby appeared more inviting, a stylish atrium of tall windows and expansive marble floors.

Although only in his thirties, Simon Lutz already had the posture of an old man. He had a smallish pinched face and the deep-set eyes of a miserly goblin.

"Detective Krieg," he called out, his voice booming across the lobby. He approached her, his hand extended at arm's length. One consequence that came with Shelley's height: It announced who she was to anyone who had received even a cursory description.

"My client didn't exaggerate," the lawyer said. "You truly do have a compelling presence." Their hands met and shook.

"I prefer 'force of nature.' This is my colleague, Yasmira Tamer. She works in the crime lab."

"Senior technician."

Simon shook Mira's hand. "Thanks for agreeing to meet me here. I'm always caught up in a swirl of business at the courts, and they've got plenty of private booths for formal negotiations. Let's hunt down a chamber and talk."

"Lead the way," Shelley said.

He walked in front of them while talking over his shoulder. "I can see why Rafael blabbered so much in the interrogation room. One look at you and I'm feeling coerced."

"One comment on my height is all you get," Shelley said.

Lutz opened the door to a cramped meeting room filled by a round table encircled by four chairs, with barely any space to squeeze past. After some squirming, they each settled into a seat.

"Mr. Lutz ..." Shelley began.

"Simon."

Shelley had expected this meeting would be adversarial, but the lawyer appeared relaxed. "Simon ..." Shelley started again but, before she could continue, Mira took over.

"We've got this for you," she said. She opened the sleeve of an accordion file and extracted a swath of papers. "When he was being detained as a suspect, Mr. Hooks urinated on the carpet in his building's hallway."

"And on his clothes, as he informed me," Lutz said. "When the responding officer was leading my client out, one Detective Atchison ordered him kept nearby. They parked him at the top of the stairs, where he waited. And waited. Until he pissed on himself."

"We cut out a piece of the rug," Mira said. "I took it to the crime lab, ran an organic extraction, passed it through a filter column, then ran the eluate in an LC."

"You don't testify often in court, do you?" Lutz asked. When Mira was unresponsive, he gave a magician's wave of his hands. "In English, please?"

"I identified a chemical of interest. GHB, gamma-hydroxy-butyrate, sometimes called Liquid X. It's a powerful sedative and can produce situational amnesia."

Lutz blinked a lot as he listened. When Mira finished her explanation, he said, "So, essentially, you're validating my client's story?"

"That's correct."

"That's the good news," Shelley said. "However, the rug was not formally collected as evidence. Excuse me, I mean not collected as formal evidence."

"And yet you processed it," Lutz said. "Then you bypassed channels to meet with me. Curiouser and curiouser."

Mira passed the jacket of evidence to Lutz. "You can use this information to insist that they test his clothes—which *were* formally logged into evidence."

"And why don't you do that yourselves?" Lutz asked. "Better yet, why don't you just drop the charges now?"

"Can I speak confidentially?" Shelley asked.

"No," Lutz said. "We're not sharing attorney-client privilege. For me to act as though your statements are off the record is not in the best interests of the client whom I do represent."

"I understand," Shelley said. "However, I'm risking my career coming straight to you."

"I appreciate that. But my appreciation is all you're going to get."

"Really? What I have to offer you is explosive and I need you to promise not to use it unless it's absolutely necessary."

"That much I can do. However, the term 'absolutely necessary' means something different to me than it does to you."

Shelley looked Lutz directly in the eye. "I believe some of my fellow officers are involved."

"Involved in framing my client?"

"I believe police killed Keshawn."

"And two others," Mira added.

Shelley shot a glare at Mira. Cassidy was not part of these negotiations. "*One* other. A man named Ernesto Grey in Maryland."

The lawyer's face bunched up. "Why not take this to your internal affairs?"

"I'll go to them when I have something concrete," Shelley said.

"Shit and double-shit." Lutz looked at the packet as though it were a puddle of toxic waste. "What's your game here? I'm virtually a minimum-wage lawyer. Okay, that's not true, but it's crap money for the hours I put in. Are you stiffing me with some half-formed mega-corruption conspiracy not even good enough for your own investigators? And, in the meantime, I'm supposed to just leave my client hanging? What exactly do you expect me to do?"

"This is what I expect," Shelley said. "We are risking our careers and lives here. If Mira and I turn up dead in the next 24 hours, we're relying on you to save your client from a prison term for a crime he did not commit. In the meantime, keep him in the hospital prison ward. Don't let him get sent to holding. The welcome-to-lock-up attack he received was part of a plan to kill him."

Lutz glared at Shelley. "If the police have made him a target, is he really safe in the prison hospital ward?"

Shelley realized Lutz was right. "Any visitor is supposed to have an escort. But you've got a point. That's not enough. I'll make sure he's better guarded."

Lutz clenched his hand into a claw and shook it as he spoke. "Shit! You come here and conjure up some evil cop cabal and you think this measly folder detailing some chemical analyses is enough to protect my client's interests, to keep him alive, and to set him free when I've got the DC Metro police force out to get him?"

"Do you have a tape recorder with you?" Shelley asked.

"Yes."

"I'll make a statement on tape. The same statement I'll repeat in court, if necessary. I will detail my suspicions and the evidence I've gathered thus far. Only ..." she chose her words carefully, tailoring them in legal language, " ... since my account contains conjecture that may unjustly implicate others ... you must give me your word you will not exploit the contents of my statement unless there is a legal necessity."

Lutz nodded. "Unless and until. You have my word I will employ this material only under exigent circumstances."

"That circumstance being my death," Shelley said.

"She means if we're both dead." Mira added. Shelley squeezed her hand.

Lutz looked at Mira's trembling figure, studied Shelley's grim expression. He said, "I don't exactly believe what-all you're telling me, but *you* sure as hell believe it."

He extracted a microcassette recorder from his pocket and pressed RECORD.

41

SHELLEY AND MIRA were on foot, searching for a pay phone. Shelley wore a puffy jacket, zipped up, hood in place. She could have passed for a tall man. That's what she wanted, a bit of anonymity. Mira walked alongside swaddled in a Mexican blanket borrowed from Shelley's back seat, a make-do wrapping for her thin clothes. Mira called it a "sloppy serape."

They needed to hunt down the right sort of phone, one far from prying eyes, certainly away from the security cameras that surrounded the courthouse buildings. In this age of cellular communication, payphones had begun disappearing and those that remained were often gutted. Still, in DC, government buildings were often located a short stroll from bleak poverty: rundown projects with surrounding wasteland courtyards and one public telephone to serve those tenants who couldn't afford a landline or a cellular.

They didn't take the car. Shelley wanted no witnesses who might note the license plate. If questioned, whoever saw them would describe a tall man and a Mexican lady.

Shelley rubbed her gloved fingers over a pair of quarters to smudge whatever prints remained. After connecting to the operator, she spoke in a rasping, husky voice, asking to be transferred to the health-care facility at DC Central Detention.

A receptionist answered. "Detention Ward."

"You all got that killer Rafael Hooks in your care?" Shelley asked with a growl.

The receptionist stated she could neither confirm nor deny this.

"You tell that fucking murderer that he is suing good hard-working police, trying to suck off our pensions. You tell him the cops are coming for him." Shelley hung up.

"You watch too many movies, Shel."

"That should put a stop to any police who try paying him a visit."

They passed a brick wall tagged by graffiti declaring "Live By The Gun."

"Isn't it sad?" Mira asked. "With all of this town's history and how it's going to hell?"

"'Cause of us Negroes? Up at American, I had this criminology professor, Dr. Therwald. During one lecture, he showed us slides of American currency. He said the Vice President of the man on the nickel shot and killed the man on the ten-dollar bill. The man on the twenty shot and killed one man and dueled with a dozen others. He carried three bullets in his body. The man on the five took a bullet to the brain. The man on the fifty worked for the man on the five. He was a drunk who became a hero for his willingness to lead his men to be butchered. It's been guns, guns, guns forever. It's who we are."

Shelley pressed the car-key button. The Malibu chirped to greet their arrival.

42

PARKED BUMPER TO bumper along both curbs, cars lined the Georgetown street, leaving a narrow passage for moving traffic. Sheena Vance lived in this upscale neighborhood in one of a long series of linked row houses. Every dead garden looked the same, all color bled from each slice of terraced lawn so that, on this gray autumn afternoon, one residence mirrored the next, creating an ever-diminishing succession of bricks, windows, and trimming. Shelley peered out of the car window, searching for addresses. Few owners tagged their residences with numbers or plaques, choosing confusion as a form of privacy and prestige. Finally, Shelley located a house number: Sheena's place. Made sense. Her neighbors could live in obscurity, but her clients would need some indicator.

Sheena greeted them at the door wearing a kimono decorated with a cascade of hummingbirds and cherry blossoms. She had downy peach-colored hair, the same delicate shade that appeared in her eyebrows and decorated her lips. Her face was long and handsome. She seemed model-tall, an illusion enhanced by her three-inch heels.

Shelley zipped down her jacket. Mira unwrapped her poncho.

Sheena performed a slow dip of her head, taking in her visitors. "You two make for quite the tag team."

"I'm Detective Shelley Krieg." Shelley offered her hand. "Lieutenant Salvatore Morretti steered me your way."

Sheena looked at the proffered hand as though it were a sordid object, an unrefined form of greeting. She kissed Shelley's cheek, lingering to leave behind a hint of her perfume. Then she swept her arm, inviting them into her living room. "Shelley Krieg. I know who you are. Sal often sings your praises. I think he has a thing for you."

"My name is Yasmira Tamer," Mira said. "A colleague of Detective Krieg's."

Sheena seemed guided by her shoulders, initiating a pivot with a twist of her upper torso. Her kimono followed, flowing with her movements.

The living room was decorated with Mapplethorpe prints, male muscled torsos, each of the pictures cropped to remove the head and reveal only the uppermost slivers of pubic hair.

"I expect five hundred apiece for the half hour or eight hundred for the full hour," Sheena said. "I service most specialties, some at additional cost. I prefer using my own toys; you'll find I maintain a satisfying selection. If you have a C.I.

sheet, I like to read before I sign. Tea? I have my kettle on the stove and keep a stock of stimulating herbs."

"I need to talk to you about the services you exchange for acting as a paid informant," Shelley said.

"Are you here as investigators or did you come to have fun?"

"Can't it be both?" Mira asked. Shelley shot her a glare.

Sheena plopped down into a scoop rattan chair and crossed her legs. Her eyes became tiny cold marbles. "Sal told me someday police would be dropping by with questions. He advised me to take the Fifth."

"We have no interest in interfering with your business," Shelley said. "We're not going to write a report or take you in."

"My record is clean. Never an arrest. I have influential friends in the department. So please don't think of messing with me."

"No messing, you have my word," Shelley said. "I'm investigating another matter. Some other paid informants have been killed."

"Should I be concerned about my own well-being?"

Shelley hadn't considered this. Sheena was not on the list, but did that mean she was safe? "I don't know, but perhaps it's best you find a place to escape to for a couple of nights."

From the kitchen, the sound of a kettle trilling. "Are you certain you won't take tea?"

"None for me," Shelley said.

"Do you have damiana leaf?" Mira asked.

"Of course." Sheena strode into her kitchen, her high heels clacking on the tiles. With floorboard accent lights flooding her kimono, it appeared see-through, her broad hips and firm torso ghostly visible. Sheena flicked off the flame on her stove's burner, grabbed a pair of mugs from her cabinet, and set them in saucers. After collecting her tea-tin, she dropped bags into the mugs and filled them with steaming water. "Sugar? Sweet'N Low?" she asked Mira.

"No, neither. Thanks."

Sheena ferried the mugs back to her living room. Shelley leaned against the wall, fidgeting, impatient. Mira took a seat, scooting her feet up into a scoop chair. She thanked Sheena for the tea and cupped the mug in her hands, allowing its warmth to radiate through her.

"Did Sal send you here?" Sheena asked.

"Yes," Shelley lied.

"I like Sal. He's so gentle and sensitive—but you probably already know that."

Mira whispered, "Sal? *Click?*"

Sheena sat again in her rattan chair and took a sip of her tea. "So, tell me, what is it that I could possibly know that Sal couldn't help you with?"

With that deft maneuver delivered in a purring voice, Sheena had called Shelley's bluff. If Click had sent them, Shelley would already have all the information she needed.

"We're investigating something called snitch-snatch," Shelley said.

"I'm not a snitch and I'm not a snatch. I've never had to inform for my payments and to call a woman a snatch is plain vulgar."

"Very good point," Mira said, wagging a finger at Shelley.

Shelley ignored the criticism. "As you stated, Ms. Vance, there is little you can tell me that I couldn't get from Click— from Sal. So let's start with what we do know and go from there. We know you signed off as a confidential informant for Morretti."

"And others. My services promote good police work. As Sal explained it, the officer develops important information to solve a case or plan a raid. Instead of the money going to a sketchy street snitch, it comes to me. The police cash in their chits and I provide them with their reward."

"Three confidential informants have been killed."

"Three?"

"Do you know Ernesto Grey, Keshawn Davies, or Cassidy Higgins?"

"No. Were they pros?"

Shelley hadn't considered that angle. Her instinct told her they weren't male prostitutes, but she wanted Sheena to talk. "We believe so."

"I don't know many male hustlers, but ... tell me what I can do to help."

"Do you know Josef Serov? A Russian."

"No."

"Kris Atchison."

"Sal's partner? Sal's talked about him but we've never met."

"Jess Usher?"

Sheena shook her head.

"Cap Duggan?"

"No. But then if I don't have to sign a C.I. sheet, I usually receive an alias. Even when they're famous, even those whom I do recognize, I pretend not to."

"Do you have other cops?"

"I won't name names. If I don't maintain a measure of secrecy, I have no business."

Shelley thought, *Time to sell a lie.* "Ms. Vance, there's a chance that Sal is in danger. Whatever you tell me can help him. If we can keep this between us, if we can keep other investigators out of this, we won't expose your business."

Frown lines seemed never to have visited Sheena's face. Even now, she showed her concern with a sidewise stare. "In our last three visits, Sal paid me out of pocket. He seemed nervous. He told me he's a snitch now. He talked about running off to Tahiti, asking me to come along. He said it like a joke, putting himself down, 'the fat slob and the lady,' but it came off sort of desperate. And that's about it. I would help you more if I could. He doesn't talk much about his cop life." After a moment, she added, "I see a lot of clients, but Sal is special."

43

When he'd received a citation for jaywalking, Billy Olsen had given his address as the Evarts Street African Methodist Episcopal (AME) church. Now Mira waited behind in the car half a block away from the church. The idling engine and blasting heaters offered warmth. Shelley promised she'd be right back. This would be a routine check, she said; there hadn't been a homeless shelter operating at the AME site for years.

The crumbling two-story church had once been magnificent. Flying arches braced its tall walls. Its roof was pitched high, an arrow stabbing at the foot of heaven. Its famed teardrop-shaped stained-glass windows were long gone, rescued and spirited away by preservationists.

It had a venerable history. Constructed as a Quaker meeting house in the 1850s, it was commandeered by the military and transformed into a recovery hospital during the Civil War. In 1875, a fire gutted its interior, leaving behind a brick shell. Elders from the AME Church bought and restored the building in the 1890s, bringing it a new glory that lasted for nearly a century. In the mid-1980s, its socially minded congregation voted to convert the first floor into a kitchen and a shelter for the homeless.

As a lack of funding became an ever-constant crisis, the facilities slowly surrendered to leaching lead pipes and crumbling lead paint. After the turn of the millennium, the city stopped turning a blind eye to its poisons and molds and officially condemned the building. The congregation merged with a nearby church. Some of the homeless stayed behind. At first, the squat stayed peaceable, but soon the more aggressive hoods and addicts settled in, mixing with the destitute. For those living on the street its ruins became a refuge of last resort.

The church grounds were now sealed off by a chain-link fence topped with a twisting spiral of barbed wire. The fence extended into a vacant lot, disappearing amid the overgrowth. Shelley followed its perimeter, certain she would run across an entry point, a breach.

With daylight savings over, night had descended an hour earlier. At 6:00 P.M. an unsettling dusk blanketed the area. Clouds blotted out any hope of moonlight. City workers had yet to adjust the timers on the streetlights to the new schedule, leaving the sodium lamps unlit. The darkness in the wild growth was as deep as that of a storybook forest.

Shelley illuminated her path with an LED flashlight that fit snugly in her palm. She hated using it. It announced she was coming and it occupied a hand that could hold her firearm.

Her other hand busied itself fighting low-hanging branches. Denuded by the brisk autumn, stems reached for her face like attacking talons.

Passing a skeletal elm, she encountered a well-trampled portion of fence that lay fully collapsed. An orange extension cord snaked across it—the squatters had found a way to free-load off of some neighbor's current.

A wide sweep of cement steps led up to the second-floor chapel, the church's main entrance. There, the doors were well sealed with tall panels of plywood bolted in place. Instead of searching for a loose board, Shelley used the electrical extension cord as her guide, following its track downwards into the well of a doorless entryway.

The first floor of the church resembled a basement, its low ceiling supported by a forest of pillars.

The floor had teeth. Shards of glass lay strewn about, the jagged fragments of liquor bottles and crack vials. Some conscientious Samaritan had herded discarded hypodermics into a single jagged pile.

The original extension cord came to an end where it joined to an outlet strip. There, eight sockets sprouted further cables that spider-legged in all directions, including one that went straight up.

Shelley looked around her. The homeless wore blankets like buffalo hides, bundled up so only their faces showed. Their breath steaming, they marched about, a legion of shaggy monks, keeping in motion to stave off the chill. A feral child flitted between support columns. She paused beneath a hanging light long enough for Shelley to get a solid look at her. Her face was smudged with grime, her lips cracked, her eyes a shade of blue so light they seemed nearly absent of color.

The child maneuvered behind an old lady who sat huddled on the floor, her clawlike hands soaking in the small sphere of warmth radiating from a space heater. Shelley pawed through her pants pocket, found a ten-dollar bill. She set it in the old woman's hand. The lady pinched the bill for a moment, then let it drop to the floor. She directed her gaze at Shelley, but her focus remained a long ways distant.

"I'm looking for Billy Olsen," Shelley said.

The child raised her index finger to her lips and then pointed overhead. She mouthed the word "up," the "P" popping on her lips.

The staircase was a twist of metalwork, a corkscrew rising up through a hole in the ceiling. Shelley's shoes struck the steps as she ascended, making heavy bonging sounds like a farrier's hammer striking an anvil.

The church's nave stood broad and tall, steeped in darkness. Wind gusted through the frames that had previously held stained glass. The wooden pews once seated hundreds. Now most were splintered, and some had buckled and collapsed into a jumble of planks. In warmer seasons, the few undamaged pews served as make-do cots, but on nights like these, the cold chased the squatters to the floor below.

Shelley swung her flashlight beam up and down the walls, shadows spiking and collapsing. With the front door of the church sealed, the only exits were the several staircases spiraling down like drill bits boring their way to the basement.

Across all of the second floor, only the altar was lit. A utility lamp dangled from the harp-shaped book-holder of a lectern. From that direction came a snapping, crunching sound. Shelley cut her flashlight and maneuvered closer, slipping behind a pillar. She peered around its edge.

There, on the altar, the blond assassin knelt over the body of Billy Olsen. Using sturdy clippers Josef Serov chopped efficiently and brutally through Billy's ribs. An automatic lay on the floor to Serov's side. Shelley drew her cell phone from her coat pocket and snapped a shot. Then she selected Kent from her contact list and sent him the photo.

Serov hadn't responded to her presence or to the sounds of her climbing the stairs. Perhaps he considered her movements part of the background noise of the wandering homeless. Time to change that. She pocketed the phone and drew her gun.

Shelley stepped out from behind the column. "Josef!" she said, aiming her pistol at him.

Josef Serov looked up from his crouched position and glared at her like a cobra coiled and ready to strike.

"Face down! Face down on the floor!" Shelley ordered. Ballinger had warned her that Serov didn't speak English, but she suspected that even if he had understood the words, he would still have refused to obey them.

With his head still, his eyes swept the room from side to side. Shelley suspected he was searching for her back-up.

Then from a dark corner, a set of footfalls. A shadowy figure rushed to the front stairwell—Usher. His shoes clattered against the steps as he descended. With Shelley's attention diverted for a moment, Serov swept his free hand toward his gun.

"No! Nein!" Shelley struggled to come up with a single Russian word. She nodded her gun to convey her meaning, then remembered. "Nyet! Nyet!"

Serov froze, the rib-choppers in his hand dripping blood. Slowly, he lowered the loppers as though setting them down. Their jaws slid around the power cord. He cut the light.

Shelley backed away, blindly groping for some safe cover, sliding behind a pillar just as Serov's gun spit out three shots in her direction. In the brief flashes she could see him firing, gun held at arm's length as he ran.

These weren't intended to be kill shots, merely protective fire as he ran for cover.

The gun flashes faded from the wells of her retinas, leaving behind a complete darkness, absolute and lethal. Shelley listened for movement. The shots had stirred those on the floor below; they rustled like nervous cattle on the verge of stampeding.

Her flashlight had a metal clip. She snipped this over her jacket sleeve, then as quietly as she could, she removed her jacket. With her decoy assembled, she flipped on the light. As she dangled that sleeve around the corner of the pillar, three shots were fired. Two bullets hit the fabric, and one smashed the light.

Jesus, Shelley thought. *That's tight shooting. If my arm had been in that sleeve he'd have blasted off my hand.*

She didn't want to lower her gun, not even for the moments it would take to put on her jacket, so she slung it over her neck, making a loose knot with her free hand.

She heard a magazine clattering on the floor and, a moment later, a fresh jacket of bullets snapping in place. He had fired six bullets, and perhaps more before she'd arrived. Had he spent his ammo? A six-shell automatic? No, he was just making sure he had a full magazine ready. Maybe he'd switched to an oversized clip he'd kept on hand.

She pressed against the pillar. She could not imagine anyone maneuvering across the decrepit floor without eliciting a creak. Her best opportunity would come when he revealed his position with a stray sound before creeping up and getting her in his crosshairs. Still, what had Ballinger said? *When you think you trapped him in a corner you'll find he's tap-tapping the back of your shoulder.*

She held her breath. The noises from below had ceased. A gust of wind streaked through the windows and buffeted the walls. Only these sounds, no more. A minute passed. She took out her cell phone, opening it, suddenly very conscious of how much light it emitted.

Then ... the quick clatter of footfalls clanking down the metal stairs. He had been moving silently—in the direction of escape.

Shelley used her cell phone's light to guide her way forward down the aisle between the pews. When she came to the altar she could hear Olsen's soft gurgling breath. He was still alive. She felt his neck pulse: thumping, pounding like the fist of someone buried alive and beating against the lid of his pine box.

She dialed 911, told the operator the address, and requested a trauma unit. Then she hung up. She knelt by Olsen, uncertain of what she could do to help. She could only imagine the futility of performing CPR on a half-opened chest. She squeezed his hand for comfort. His gurgling breath stopped. Then, from outdoors, the squeal of rubber on pavement followed by the pop-pop of two gunshots, more screeching rubber and finally the grinding metal of a crash. *Mira.*

44

SHELLEY HURTLED BLINDLY through thick shadows in the direction of the spiral staircase, slamming her kneecap against its handrail when she arrived. She hobbled down the steps to the first floor. The squatters had scattered, hiding, crouched in nooks, cramming themselves into the recesses of cobwebbed closets or crawling beneath the slats of their flimsy makeshift shelters. Even under the threat of gunfire, they had nowhere else to flee. In the stampede, someone had trampled over and smashed the old lady's heater.

Shelley's path across this floor was lamplit, so she soon made her way out onto the grounds, plunging headlong through the clawing branches, rushing out into the street, stopping at the curb where Mira had parked. The streetlamps were now on.

On the sidewalk, two bullet casings. A block and a half distant, Shelley's Malibu had rammed into a tree.

Ignoring the throbbing ache in her knee, she sprinted the distance. As she approached the Malibu she saw that its back window had been blasted out. Nothing remained but a ragged fringe. The front window had also been shattered by bullets. Broken glass lay sprayed across the car's hood.

Mira sat slumped low in the driver's seat draped by a now-deflated airbag. As Shelley grabbed the door handle, Mira bolted up. "I have pepper spray!"

"It's me," Shelley said as reassuringly as she could. "Are you okay?"

Pellets of shattered glass littered the front seat; some were strewn in Mira's lap and hair. Dribbles of blood ran from scratches on her scalp, their trails looping around her eyes and trickling down her cheeks. "Not really," she replied. "How are you?"

Mira pulled back her seatbelt as though she was ripping off a scab. "These belts really pack a punch, you know? I've got a bruise in the shape of a sash." She grabbed the door frame and pulled herself out of the car. Wobbling to her feet, she fell against Shelley.

Shelley wrapped her arms around her. "I'll get you to the hospital ..."

"No. It looks worse than it is. It feels like I've got a five-foot-five-inch charley horse. I can shake it off."

"I'm sorry. I was pinned inside the church. At first I couldn't escape, then ..."

"No need to apologize, Shel. Jeez."

Mira limped around a bit, trying to work the spasm out of her legs. "I heard the gunfire. I wanted to leave, but I thought I'd wait, maybe you'd come stumbling out, hurt. I didn't want to abandon you. And then came this crazy blond guy, gun in hand. I burned rubber, trying to put as much distance between us as I could. I saw him in the rearview mirror, taking aim. He fired two shots—both went through the back and front windows. With the windshield all cracked, I couldn't see right and swerved into this tree. After that I thought it was safer to stay in the car, play dead, and not move."

"You did good," Shelley said. She squeezed Mira tightly enough to suffocate her.

"Tell me I'm still beautiful."

"Always and forever." She slung her jacket around Mira, who smudged blood and tears from her cheeks and shook glass chips from her hair.

"They've upped the ante," Shelley said. "We've got to change our game plan. I'll drive us to my place, where we can pick up your car. Then we'll both head somewhere safe, someplace where they won't know to find us." She looked over her wrecked vehicle. "If I can get my car started, that is."

45

THE 911 CALL, the gunshots—sirens answered their summons. Shelley wrapped her jacket around her fist and punched out the remainder of the front and back windshields, figuring that she and Mira were more likely to be pulled over if the car had smashed windshields than if it had no windshields at all. She swept glass pellets from the car seats. She climbed inside, gave the ignition a turn. It complained with a guttural groan, then started. She backed the car up, freeing it from the tree. Its grille was dented and its hood buckled. Its passenger door had fallen out of line and refused to open.

Mira clambered over Shelley to take a seat. She borrowed Shelley's jacket to wipe away more glass that had fallen off the shuddering dashboard. Then she hugged the jacket tightly as Shelley drove off.

Shelley trembled more from adrenaline than from the cold. "Mira, when you saw Josef in the rearview mirror aiming at the car—was he kneeling or crouching?"

Mira shut her eyes for a moment. "No, he was standing, legs spread shoulder-width, gun at his hip."

"How far were you away at the time of the shots?"

"Half a soccer field, I'd guess."

Shelley acted out drawing her gun, raising and lowering it to different heights. "The bullets went through the back windshield and then the front windshield. That's a straight shot from a low vantage point. It means he drew his gun, didn't bother to raise it, firing from the hip, Wild West style. At fifty yards, he managed to pop off two shots, both coming within an inch of killing you. That's some fancy shooting."

Shelley blasted the heaters to full. The hot air smelled of engine oil mixed with brake, steering, and transmission fluids. She imagined her car's every reservoir leaking, leaving behind a Hansel and Gretel trail of dots leading the police from the site of the accident to her house.

46

WHEN SHELLEY DROVE into her garage and cut the engine, her shattered car gave a parting snort as though it had breathed its last and welcomed death as an end to its misery.

Shelley made a long sweeping assessment of the inside of her garage. Cassidy still lay hidden in the space above the door. The light was on only because the door was open.

"We'll stay at the Rocco Motor Inn, 43rd and East Capitol," she said. "About a mile and a half from here. It's two blocks from the Sixth District Station. Sometimes the Metro police use it to house visiting officers. It should be safe. Head to your place and pack. I've got a couple of errands to do. I'll meet you there in half an hour."

They got out of the car and shared a quick embrace. Mira stepped into the driveway.

"Bye, kiddo," Shelley said.

The two friends stared at each other for several awkward moments until Shelley pressed the remote for the garage door. It scrolled down, shutting out Mira.

The garage light cut. Stashing the corpse above the garage door seemed smart at the moment, but now with the door closed she stood in the dark. In retrospect, it had been a foolish mistake. The police would visit sooner or later, friendly or with a warrant. She'd guaranteed that when she sent the 911 call from her phone while at the AME church, where dozens of homeless had witnessed a giant black woman fleeing the scene. Maybe someone caught her license tag when her car nosed the tree. Or maybe they'd follow the drip-drip spilling from her car's guts. She reached through the empty windshield and tugged the knob to switch on the car's headlights.

Her garage seemed small, cage-like. She switched on her cell phone, accessed her contacts, and chose Ruth Ann Baylor, her next-door neighbor. At eighty-three, Ruth Ann had a sharp mind trapped in an arthritic body. A home help aide visited her twice a week on the days her children couldn't drop by. Ruth Ann's movement had become so impaired she never ventured from her first floor. Her basement had an entry from the alleyway. Although it had once been a garage, it was now filled with a lifetime of clutter.

"Ruth Ann?"

"Shelley, child! It's been ages."

"I'm sorry, Ruthie, I get so caught up in my work."

"I was like you once. So long ago. A different life."

"Ruthie? I was wondering if I could store something in your garage? Just for a couple of days."

"I suppose ... but you have so much space with you being there all alone ..."

Shelley hoped to avoid a you-ought-to-have-kids lecture. "It's a surprise for someone. All wrapped up. I can't have them walking in on it."

"Won't fit under a bed?"

"A lawn mower."

"The sit-on kind? I remember your momma borrowing one of them. Is Della coming for a visit?"

"No, Mom's all tied up with her life in Atlanta."

"A shame. You tell her Ruthie Ann sends her kisses and a big hello."

"I will."

"I guess I can loan you my remote to open the garage door for you. I don't get down there much."

"That will be fine, that will be perfect. Thanks, Ruthie."

With the house door open, Shelly flipped the switch to turn off the Malibu's headlights.

47

As SHELLEY HAULED the body bag down to her basement, out the back door, and into Ruth Ann's garage, she considered her situation. She had been running an off-the-books investigation. Now the game had turned even more deadly. She couldn't play any longer. If she'd brought in help when she collected the names, perhaps Olsen would still be alive. She had placed herself, Mira, Kent, and Kimmy in the gunsights of killers.

When she met up with Mira, they'd go to the FBI with the information they had. Or else the city attorney. Or IAD. Whoever would listen.

She dreaded the next few days. She'd become a police snitch, ratting out fellow officers. An official investigation would expose her fast-and-loose operation: dumping evidence, the body and the carpets, breaking into the crime scene, not reporting murders. *My career is over.*

Shelley didn't know when she'd return home. Until things settled down, she and Mira would live at the Rocco. She stuffed a gym bag with the items she deemed essential: several changes of clothes and undergarments, toiletries, her laptop, the pages of the case file and, most importantly, her automatic and an extra clip. She slung the bag over her shoulder and headed into the garage, where she'd learn whether her car had the heart to make one last trip.

Cutting the house lights, she stepped into the pure darkness of the garage. She felt for the car's door handle and cracked the door open, metal crunching against crumpled metal. Sliding into the driver's seat, she flipped on the headlights. As she put her key in the ignition, her mind conjured up images from films where hit men used car bombs. She dismissed the thought as paranoia. When would they have had the opportunity to plant it? She had started the car back at the AME church without incident.

Another idea struck her. She got out, knelt down, and peeked at the wheel well. There she encountered a magnetic transponder. Someone had been tracking her every move. That's how they'd located Cassidy's body. That's how Serov knew to stake out Keshawn's murder scene.

She removed the device. At least now they wouldn't know to follow her to the motel.

Her cell phone rang. She didn't recognize the number. "Hello?"

Kent spoke, his voice a harsh whisper. "Shel! They're in my apartment. I can hear them now. They're knocking over my furniture, tossing my things around."

"Are you and Kimmy safe?"

"We were visiting my next-door neighbor, my girlfriend, when they broke in. My gun and my cell phone are next door. We're laying low, staying quiet, waiting on the police. When I make out the report, I'll try to keep you and your troubles out of it, but seriously—you're not my first priority. I can hear them. They've opened the door to the hall."

Over the phone line, Shelley heard a bell buzz.

"Kimmy, don't answer the doorbell," her father said.

His voice louder: "*No, Kimmy, don't answer the door.*" The line clicked dead.

Don't answer the door. With those words, Shelley felt herself sliding down a chute into a dark pit ... 3:36 A.M. *The memory again.* With a gasp Shelley awoke to the sound of her doorbell. *Don't answer the door.* She stirred in her bed, her head buzzing. *I had a Manhattan and how many beers?* She grabbed her gray sweats from where they lay draped over a chair.

The doorbell again. "I'm coming."

Don't answer the door.

She tottered toward the door. The heater hummed. The refrigerator rumbled. The house's alarm light maintained its slow, steady blink.

Shelley *had* to allow the story to replay. She *had* to open the door, invite in those who had invaded her house, who drugged her, who murdered Cassidy. This time she would let the memory be in charge. She wouldn't look away.

Giving up control made it all the more terrifying. She felt herself being pulled to the front door.

She passed through her kitchen. Her living-room curtains were wide open. A dark car sat parked in front. The streetlamp cast her furniture into blocks of shadows. She peeked through the peephole but couldn't make out what she saw. She flipped on the porch light.

A voice called out. "We've got some developments in your case. We need to talk, now."

It was Click.

"You couldn't just call me?" Shelley asked.

She punched numbers on the alarm keypad, slipped the deadbolt from its lock, twisted the doorknob. The door opened.

Click brushed past her, swiveled, and then looked out the door fearfully. As Shelley turned to see what he saw, he reached over and squeezed her wrist. He wore a vinyl glove slathered with a shiny, oily substance. Shelley reflexively grabbed his gloved hand; now the ointment covered her palm. A tingle rose up through the veins in her arms. She felt her pulse thump: one, two, three ... No, it was counting down. Three, two, one ... Her eyes closed, her legs buckled. All sight and sound switched off and she remembered nothing more.

SHELLEY SAT IN her car, her throat tight, her lips pressed closed, her breath snorting in clouds of condensation. *Click. It had been Click all along.*

She remembered Kent and dialed dispatch. "This is Detective Shelley Krieg. An officer is under attack, 1730 Monroe,

Northwest. The Belham Apartments. Third floor, I don't know the apartment number. Sergeant Kent Bellotti."

"We've already sent a vehicle. They've reported on scene."

Her phone beeped, a call trying to get through. "Thanks," she said, switching to her other line, thinking Kent was contacting her to give her an update. "Hello?"

"Shelley." Click's voice. "Get out of the house now. They're coming to kill you."

48

In her tenderfoot year on patrol, Officer Shelley Krieg sustained a daily onslaught of mind-numbing, spirit-bruising encounters on the street, its morally distorted world colliding with her entrenched idealism. The police were like wolves, picking off the easy prey. The most reprehensible criminals stayed free by ratting out the minor players.

Some crimes were overlooked while others met with brutal force. A twelve-year-old who disrespected a patrol car would be hurled face first to the pavement. A pimp who beat his girls would make an easy twenty by squealing on some loser stupid enough to be caught holding in a school zone.

Up was down, down was up. Harmless teens play-acted as hoodlums, dressed for banging and sporting double-barreled eye-fucks. Gangster rap played like theme songs.

In the midst of this, residents tried to lead normal lives, neighbor watching out for neighbor, kids gathering in areas safe enough to play in. Everyone, the holy and the hoods, struggled to get by on not enough.

Along with the tribulations provided by the brutish streets, Shelley was routinely cut down by her partner, Officer Salvatore Morretti. Only four years her senior, he was given the task of breaking her in. He peppered her with insults and slurs, both large and small. When she complained, he told her to "man up" and take it. He was "learning her to grow a pair."

Finally, she couldn't take it anymore. She reported the harassment to her captain, meeting with him in his office.

"Since I've been paired with Officer Morretti, he has repeatedly hurled racist remarks and sexual innuendo at me."

"Are you requesting a reassignment?" Captain Partch had asked.

"I want him to stop."

"Are you making a formal complaint?"

"Unofficial."

With Shelley's response, Partch relaxed. "Did he use the n-word?"

"No, but he has used the b-word and c-word, among others."

"Take a seat." Partch headed out to the squad room.

Shelley didn't want to sit. She wanted to be the tallest person in the room. She backed up against the wall and folded her arms, pulling them in tightly against her chest.

Click entered the office and sat. The arms of the chair neatly hugged his wide rear.

"Officer Morretti," Partch said, "Officer Krieg has complained to me that you have repeatedly directed toward her person insults and obscenities of a racist and sexist nature."

Click looked Shelley over, top to bottom, as though he had never taken her measure before.

"Specifically?" Click asked.

"The b-word and the c-word," the captain said.

"And I'm sure I've used the d-word a few times." When both looked at him with question marks on their faces, he clarified, "Dyke. Not that I've got anything against dykes. Is this serious? Look at her, captain. She's a freaking mountain. How am I going to hurt her with a few words?"

"Officer Morretti," Partch said, "think carefully and then confirm my suspicions. Are you an idiot?"

Click gritted his teeth and nodded. "Yes, sir, I am."

"Are you an asshole?"

"That just about sums me up."

"If Officer Krieg were pinned down by gunfire, would you rush in to help her?"

"Damned right, I would."

"Officer Krieg," Partch summed up, "Morretti is an outstanding officer. You have the right to file a formal complaint. Don't."

Krieg trembled with anger. Partch had made it clear: *She* was the one in the wrong. "He could still be a good cop without being such a prick," she said.

"No," said the captain. "I believe performing those two actions at the same time is beyond Officer Morretti's capacities."

While Click had brushed off the idiot and asshole remarks, this comment hit home. "Look," he said. "I know I swear like a sailor. Hell, I *was* a sailor. But I'm not stupid and I'm not a racist."

"Is that all?" the captain asked.

"Depends," Morretti said. "Is that all you and this officer have for me?"

"No," the captain said. "Tell Officer Krieg how you got the nickname Click."

Morretti slumped his shoulders and pouted. "Aw, come on, Chief. Do I have to?"

"She's going to hear the story from someone."

"Okay," Click said, reluctantly. "I've always liked acting. Theater, high school, I was good at it. Back when I started on the force I took some lessons, night classes. And I had this monologue where I was blabbing on while pointing a revolver to my head, suicidal, playing a solitaire game of Russian Roulette. So, to get into the mood of the piece, I practiced at my desk with my service revolver—no civilians around and no ammo, of course. A fellow officer asked me if I wasn't worried whether maybe I left behind a bullet in a chamber and that I might blow my brains out of my head. I told him, 'Naw, it's empty.' Soon, whenever they passed my desk, all the other officers on the

220

floor started pointing their fingers to their heads, saying, 'Click, click. It's empty.' That's the story. Now, can I go?"

"No," Partch said. "Officer Krieg, call Officer Morretti a dickhead."

Shelley hesitated, her eyes flitting back and forth between the two. Finally she said, "Click, you're a dickhead."

Morretti was about to respond when the captain raised a hand and said, "Officer Morretti, Officer Krieg just called you a dickhead. Do you wish to file a complaint?"

"No, sir, I don't."

"Officer Krieg," Partch concluded, "you should spend your time worrying about the kiss-ass officers who won't have your backside and stop complaining about a decorated man in blue such as the asshole who sits here before you. Now you both can go."

BEFORE HE LEFT work that evening, Morretti had dropped a copy of his headshot on Shelley's desk, a black-and-white photo of an eager movie-star wannabe. On the back, it listed several jobs he'd had as an extra on film sets. He said, "My glamour shot. You know, for when you get lonely at night."

That day Shelley hated Morretti, hated Partch, hated the whole fucking police force. She told herself she had to move up the ranks, beyond the cock-swinging mentality of the patrol beat. Life would be better when she became a detective. She was certain Click was too stupid ever to pass the detective exam.

Someday, when she carried the gold badge of a detective, she would leave jerks like Morretti behind.

49

THEY'RE COMING TO kill you.

Shelley twisted the ignition key. The headlights dimmed; the starter gave a pathetic click. She pumped the gas pedal, tried again. Not even a cough. She beat her hands on the steering wheel.

No need for a defibrillator, Shelley thought. *This patient is dead.*

She considered her options. She couldn't wait for a cab. She'd have to go on foot. A mile and a half to the motel. She could manage that in a twenty-minute trot.

She cut the car lights, restoring the garage to darkness. Getting out of her car, she clicked the remote.

The garage door began rising. As the gap beneath the door reached ankle height, a pair of car headlights in her driveway flashed on. Light streamed under the door interrupted by the shadows of two pairs of legs, their outlines stretching toward her like sprung claws.

She stabbed the remote, halting the door's progress. A hail of thwump-thwumps pierced the aluminum door, gunfire from a pair of silenced pistols. The bullet holes sprouted cockeyed, tiny shafts of light.

Shelley had no time to think, only to react. Grabbing her gym bag, she rushed into her house, stumbling over the threshold as she entered and sprawling onto the floor. She kicked the door shut, then rolled over and reached up, grabbing and throwing the bolt.

She heard chatter and the rattling of her garage door. *Good,* she thought. *They're following me, I might have time to get out the back. Or did they already have the back covered?*

Maybe ... no. When they arrived in the driveway, they had probably planned to spread out. But once they overheard me banging around the car they knew they only had to stay and wait for a moment. They planted themselves in front of the garage, ready for an easy kill. But then, as the door opened, the driver turned on the headlights seconds too early.

Shelley heard a car ram her garage door. Moments later, her pursuers were inside. She scrambled to her feet and dashed into her hallway as bullets thumped against the lock on the entry to her house.

She clambered down the staircase to her basement. Above her, footsteps banged on the floorboards as the intruders spread out, exploring the rooms. She counted three sets of footsteps. *At least three.*

She unzipped her bag, seized her gun, loaded the firing chamber, and thumbed off the safety.

The upstairs became quiet. They were listening for her.

She crept toward the basement door, one silent step at a time.

She heard someone above say, "The number." A moment later, her cell phone rang.

"Downstairs!" They bolted into action the same moment she did. She had an advantage. They needed to fling open doors to search for the entry to the basement. She had only to get the hell out.

She rushed into the alleyway, her automatic raised, sweeping around, looking for a target. No one. She sprinted down the lane, then vaulted headfirst over a fence, landing with a roll against a bristly dead lawn. She ducked among the bushes.

Nearby, a dog began barking and leaping against its chain. A cavalcade of feet slapped the alleyway cement. Just as she became certain the dog would give her away, a grand chorus of fellow canines joined in. With the pandemonium of a dozen yelping animals masking the sounds of her movements, she crawled out from the bush and dashed between shadows, easily navigating the maze of her escape path. She knew this area; they didn't. As a child, she'd spent time in these yards, scaled their trees, played on their swing sets.

She climbed over another fence onto a lawn where a bulldog lunged against her, punching its paws and head against her stomach. She'd known him since he was a pup. He nuzzled against her leg. She knelt beside him, giving his scruff a brief massage.

She was in Mrs. Cantor's backyard. Seventy, an ex-school teacher, living alone. *So many widows*, Shelley thought. Her neighborhood was aging. A year ago, the last time she'd visited church, she'd seen the wizened remainders of her community and listened to their trembling voices singing hymns. All their kids had moved away.

She listened for the telltale sounds of her pursuers among the distant howls. Their hard clattering shoes seemed content to stay on the pavement. Occasionally, they stopped in unison, to listen. *Oh, shit!* Shelley thought, flicking her phone to vibrate the moment before it rang.

She heard a car screech to a halt, doors opening, then slamming.

She'd won. Her pursuers could cover a lot more territory in a car, but she could travel along near-hidden footpaths that slipped between the houses and then cut through the grounds of the Kelly Miller Recreation Center.

She dialed Mira's cell phone. She had to warn her. They'd placed a tracking device on Shelley's car and they might have done the same to Mira's. Her call went straight to voice mail.

"Ditch your car at least five blocks from the motel. Turn off your cellular. They may be tracking you. Stay calm." *Stay calm? I've pretty much guaranteed Mira will freak out.* "See you soon."

She pocketed her phone and gave a goodbye pat to the dog. Then she trotted up to the front of the Cantor house, opened its gate, and slipped out. Crossing the lawn, she began a steady jog in the direction of the Rocco Motor Inn.

50

SHELLEY PASSED A courtyard alongside the projects. Because it was early evening, the porches and windows were lit. The stinging cold had driven most everyone indoors, where they enjoyed pounding music, chirping video games, or gripping televised dramas.

Headlights beamed from beyond a corner, broadcasting the arrival of a prowling vehicle. Shelley slipped behind a shaggy evergreen. A dark blue Buick appeared, a dent on its grille, its windows wide open, its driver slowly turning his head from side to side. An automatic rested on the dashboard. At the intersection, he had three choices: turn to his left in Shelley's direction, to the right proceeding in the direction she intended to go, or continue straight ahead. He chose straight.

After the car passed, Shelley sprinted across the intersection, hoping her hunter didn't glimpse her in his rearview mirror. After a few more blocks, she slowed her pace. Up ahead, she saw the Sixth District police station. A pair of officers stood in front, huffing cold air. She slid her gun into her gym bag and raised a hand in salute.

The wind halted and the heavens opened up. A sleety rain showered from the sky.

East Capitol Street had six broad lanes with an island running down the middle. A modest amount of traffic sped in both directions. The Rocco Motor Inn stood across the street, a half block distant. Its neon signed buzzed; the final C and O were unlit.

She checked her cell to see if she had a message from Mira. With her concentration fixed on the screen, she didn't notice the dark blue Buick as it approached her from in front, hugging the gutter lane. The passenger's window rolled open. Upon looking up, for a moment Shelley felt certain she'd be shot. She drew her gun. The driver glared at her as he passed, not slowing down.

Her cell phone vibrated. She recognized the number.

"Mira?"

"We have your girlfriend," a voice said.

51

"You want her back alive?" It was Usher. "You'll need to reverse some of the damage you've done. First, keep your cell phone on. I want to hear your every footstep and I don't want you calling for help. Now, keep walking, and cross over to the Rocco. We're waiting for you."

The Rocco Motor Inn provided a drive-up covered entryway to receive its guests. A mammoth black truck idled beneath its rain-battered canopy. A pickup on steroids, it rumbled, belching out clouds from its tailpipe. Its tinted windows encased its quad cab with the wild iridescence of a scarab's shell.

Shelley approached the vehicle from behind, holding her automatic behind her back. The passenger's door cracked open. "Hop in," Click said.

Shelley directed her gun at him. He seemed unimpressed.

"Stow your weapon and hand over your phone."

"Maybe I'll keep you as hostage and trade you for Mira."

"Try that and you'll get yourself, me, and Mira killed. Come on, Shel. Put down your weapon and hop in." His face had a glint of intelligence and a determination she had never seen in him.

Through the open door, Shelley set her gun nose-down in the cup holder.

"Your phone?"

She passed Click her cellular, slung her gym bag into the foot space, and took her place in the passenger's seat.

"Buckle up," Click said. "I don't want to deliver damaged goods."

Shelley snapped her seatbelt in place.

Click spoke into her phone. "I've got her. I'll take it from here." He folded the phone shut. "They won't like me cutting the connection. They wanted to keep you on the line, to listen in. But I'll fob it off as an 'oops.' I can play dumb, I'm good at that. I've got a few things I need to share, off the record." He ground the truck into gear, then punched the accelerator. The pick-up swerved along the circular drive, splashing through the gutter as it entered East Capitol Street.

"Kidnaping? Murder?" Shelley said. "This is low, even for you, Click."

"It's not what you think. And don't call me Click. You should show me some respect. I've earned it."

"You're kidding me."

"At this point I'm the only thing keeping you alive."

"At this moment, you're the only one threatening me."

"You don't know shit, Shel." He glanced at the rearview mirror. "They're on our tail, we've got an escort. The motherfuckers won't give me an inch." He swung a left and they followed.

"Who are *they?*"

Morretti ignored her question. "To set this in perspective," he said, "three weeks back, Sergeant McArdle at Internal Affairs sat me down for a chat. During a routine audit they'd discovered I've been making creative use of the C.I. funds."

"Sheena Vance."

"IAD didn't want me. I was the little fish, their bait. They had their eyes on Atch. They laid it all out for me. To save my career I would have to worm my way into his organization. They knew he was into something big but not what.

"Atch and I are partners, but he shuts me out of most of his schemes. So I tried finding a way in. I spent a couple of weeks cozying up to him. Nothing broke until the Raffi case. When I caught Atch pocketing one of Keshawn's fingers, he opened up. He was running scared, needed my help, someone he could trust. He and some others had been working a C.I. scam, pocketing money earmarked for snitches. Just small-time thievery, perks for a thankless job, you know how it is. Then Usher recruited them to the big leagues. While working Major Crimes Narc, Usher had spent years on the Russian mob's payroll feeding leads to his unit to bust rival traffickers.

"There's this brother-in-law of the local boss, goes by the name Orloff. Recently, Usher overheard Orloff talking about a fat payload of mob money. So Usher and Atch staged a raid, snatching up the funds and leaving no witnesses. Afterwards,

they tried to pass off the heist as the work of low-level delin-
quents—some of their snitches. Grey was already listed as the
source of a half dozen busts, so they fingered him and made
sure he OD'd. But, right away, things got ugly. The mob chiefs
brought in this wacko enforcer, Serov, who likes to torture
and mutilate his victims. This created a big problem. What
acts as a warning in Russia comes across like a serial psycho
here. The last thing Atch and Usher wanted was a four-alarm
investigation, so when they took out Davies they had him
write down AZ's name, figuring AZ was a big enough player
and hard enough to find, and they could point to him as the
mastermind. And, to keep down the official heat, Usher tried
to pin the first two killings on Raffi."

"The Davies and Grey murders?"

"Right. Usher is insane, a real butcher. Atch is scared of
him. He brought me in to watch his back. Not that Atch is
much better. He swapped spots in the rotation to make sure
we caught the Keshawn case.

"Like I was saying, they tried to pin the first two murders on
Raffi and then snuff him. Only Raffi survived the hit and you
were out there announcing you didn't peg him for the killer.
Right off, Serov wanted you dead, Shel. That's nuts. I convinced
our little clique that a murdered cop invited too much heat and
thought up the idea of dumping Cassidy's body in your house to
neutralize you."

"You're working undercover and you let them kill Cassidy?"

"I swear to God, Shel, I thought they'd already offed Cassidy.
If I'd known they hadn't killed him yet, I would have broken
cover, brought in the cavalry. Now, fuck! I'm as good as respon-

sible for his murder. It all went down so fast. I had to come up with something. I thought I was saving your life."

"And when they tried to kill Raffi?"

"I didn't know that was coming. Jeez, Shel. Since Friday night I've been like you, playing catch-up, running this off the books, not exactly legal. I've been looking for a way out of this mess. And I've been trying to keep you off this case, to keep you alive. I never thought you, of all people, would dump Cassidy. Krieg not reporting a dead man in her house? Come on. Then, when you hauled off Cassidy's body and went back to the crime scene, they wanted your head again. I convinced them to bring Cassidy back to your place. But the last straw came this afternoon when you took that photo of Serov. He went berserk. Okay, so I couldn't talk them out of killing you, but I got them to hold off long enough to strong-arm you into undoing the harm you caused them."

"Have you reported any of this to IAD?"

"Raffi, the mob, the raid—I haven't told McArdle a thing. I'm just trying to get out of this with my life and my career. I suspect you're doing the same. And there's this: I once asked Atch if he didn't worry about Internal Affairs. He told me he had a source there. If that rat learns I'm playing both sides, I'm dead."

"Who was in on the raid?"

"Usher and Atch, of course. Two more from narco in PG— Mitch and Mike—I don't know their last names. They've got a couple of more in the shadows. Someone they refer to as 'chief' and a patrolman with Metro PD they call Els."

"Els?"

"Yeah. Haven't met him."

"What about Duggan?"

"Duggan is a dupe. He got placed on the Ernesto Grey case but doesn't have a clue."

"What do you know about Serov?"

"Usher has been shuttling him around, pointing out snitches, claiming they were in on the heist." Morretti's pick-up got trapped behind a pair of Metro buses. He downshifted and glanced again at the rearview mirror. "Usher has some kind of power over the guy, like his own personal, wind-up assassin. At the same time Usher is terrified of him. He's sure Serov will uncover the con. He planned to kill Serov at the AME church, only something happened."

"I happened."

"I should have guessed."

"I've wondered why Serov didn't just kill me."

"He was under orders not to. Those orders have since been rescinded."

As the light up ahead turned yellow the Metro buses powered through the intersection. Morretti slowed to a stop. The Buick pulled up directly behind them.

Click handed his cellular to Shelley. "Swap your phone's ID chip with mine. Then erase what you can on my memory card. It'll ring your number but hold my history. That'll keep them puzzled for a bit. And we'll have saved the photo of Serov in your phone's memory. Serov's crazy about that photo, you know. They assumed Kent got a copy and that's why they stormed his place. I tried to warn him but he doesn't pick up when I call. They want to get hold of your phone to check out who else you sent it to."

Shelley switched the chips and then began deleting Click's messages and canceling his speed dials. The traffic light turned green.

She spoke as she thumbed the keys. "We have to take this to the feds, Sal. We have enough to bring them down."

Click mimed a gunshot to his head. "We'll ice our careers. If everything gets out, we may go to jail. And they'll kill your girlfriend."

"Mira."

"Yeah, Mira. Spanish for 'lookie.' Shel, I never knew you were a genuine lez. I mean, I suspected it, of course, but if I had known for sure, I would never have called you a dyke. That would be insulting."

Shelley made no attempt to follow Click's moral gymnastics.

"Usher led Serov to the snitches," Click said. "They've been killed off, one by one. The only one left is Robin Hood— AZ. The Russians are frantic to find AZ, figuring he, being the last on the list, must be the one holding the stash."

Shelley forwarded the photo of Serov to Agent Ballinger. No chance he'd be working on a Sunday night, but he'd have a surprise in his box come Monday morning. She returned the phone to Click.

The truck turned onto U Street. The windshield wipers beat away the pellets of rain. Click took Shelley's weapon from the cup holder, flicked on the safety, and tucked it under his belt. He tossed a pair of Plasticuffs into her lap. "Put them on. We've got to keep up appearances. They need to believe you're my prisoner, that I can control you and walk you through all you've got to do."

"And that is?"

"We're going to the precinct station. To keep you alive I told them I saw you squirrel some files in your lockbox. I also told them you got a line on pinpointing AZ, that you'd once run him down when no one else could. They want you to write out a resignation letter explaining how you screwed up the Raffi investigation and how you broke into his apartment. You'll mention you've been suffering from depression. They'll use it as a suicide note."

Shelley slid a loop of the Plasticuffs around her wrist, yanking it tight. Then she completed the link, binding her other wrist. "They don't plan to let either me or Mira live," she said.

"No. All we can do is buy some time, look for an opening, and plan a counterattack." Click snorted. "When we broke into your house, when we knocked you out and set you in bed, Atch asked me to pull the trigger on you. To test my loyalty. I talked him down. You and I were partners once, Shel. In my book that bond transcends everything else. In my book we're amigos for life, even when I can see you hating my guts. I would never kill a friend."

"Atch is your partner."

"Fuck Atch. He's an asshole. He's out to kill both me and you. I'm supposed to help him, but I'm disposable, you know?"

"Right now, Morretti, I don't hate your guts."

"That's the nicest thing you've ever said to me."

They pulled up in front of headquarters, the Buick close behind.

Click watched in the rearview mirror as one of the Buick's back doors swung open. Atch got out. Bundled in a long winter coat, he trotted through the freezing rain to Morretti's truck.

Click rolled down his window. He handed over his phone and Shelley's gun.

"You were supposed to keep the cell phone on," Atch said.

"No, that was just until I got her in cuffs."

"You're an idiot." Atch thumbed through the cell phone screens.

"I checked for Serov's photo," Click said. "It's not in there."

"She erased it?"

"It's not in there."

"We'll deal with that later. Cut her cuffs. We can't have her walking into the station looking like a perp." Click took a thumb-sized penknife out of his pocket and popped open a blade. He severed the Plasticuffs.

"Shel?" Atch said. "I'm sorry it's got to be this way. Right now, it's you or us. Serov is not the negotiating sort. He's pretty much demanded your corpse, so we've got to play along for now. At least until we find an escape hatch and all run for the clear."

Shelley tilted her head to the side and fired both barrels of a glare. "Do you expect me to believe that?"

"Could be the Russian's not long for this world," Atch said. "So be a good soldier, do what we say, and you'll live to see your girlie-girl."

52

ATCH AND CLICK saluted the officer who babysat the metal detector. The alarm beeped. Briefly looking up from his paperback,
the officer gave a thumbs up, signaling them to enter. Shelley
passed through with her gym bag slung over her shoulder.

The three detectives entered the elevator. Atch unzipped
his jacket and flipped back the hood. He raked a comb through
his mussed hair, restoring every strand to its proper place.
Click blew into his hands, attempting to warm them. Shelley
stood stiffly, her fingers wedged beneath a gap in the shingles
of the elevator's fake wood paneling. The button reading the
number two switched off. The cab jolted to a halt and its doors
slid open.

At eight P.M. on a Sunday, the second floor was dead. The weather had shut down crime; both perpetrators and victims were burrowed deep in their respective habitats. Two detectives-on-call nested behind distant desks. They delivered up zombie stares to acknowledge the intrusion, then returned to their tasks, one gawping at his computer screen, the other slathering a baguette with brown mustard.

"Sal, try raiding the bathroom for some paper towels," Atch ordered. "I need to sponge off all this rain."

Click clenched his jaw and nodded. As he went off in search of the paper towels, Shelley flopped her gym bag on top of her desk.

"Morretti tells me you've stashed some files in your lock-box," Atch said.

"I moved them to my gym bag." Shelley unzipped and popped open her bag. She drew out a hundred pages of photocopies.

Atch shuffled through them. "You made duplicates? All this time I've spent weeding photos from the official jacket, you've been hoarding copies."

Morretti returned with a wad of paper towels. Atch used them to sop moisture from his jacket. He took off his gloves and studied his hands with a frown. He dug some fluff out from beneath a nail, then handed the photocopies to Click. "Shred these."

Click began trudging toward the shredder.

"Perhaps it's best we move to the hotbox," Shelley said. "To keep matters private."

"Lead the way."

Shelley grabbed the handle of her bag. She walked in front of Atch, smiling. She had a plan.

53

SHELLEY AND ATCH settled into seats in the interrogation room, with Shelley taking the suspect's chair. If she were to work on her computer in the big room, Atch could look over her shoulder. Here, when she opened her laptop, only she could see the screen.

Atch took out his gun, holding it at his side.

Shelley waited for her computer to boot. "Morretti explained what you want me to do," she said. "I'll start work on my good-bye note and I know a way to find AZ. But what if I could tell you there's a way out of this for you?"

Atch chuckled. "Turn myself in?"

"No. Let's say the Russian and Usher were removed from the equation. Would that let you off the hook?"

"What all did Sal tell you?"

"You know Sal, he likes to brag."

"Yeah, too much. Start typing your letter."

"Still waiting for the start screen. He told me about the big score you and Usher made, looting the Russians."

"He doesn't know jack. We were set up. The brother-in-law of the local mob boss, this guy named Orloff, staged a loud phone call, making sure Usher overheard. He described the details of the cash shipment and their problems guarding it. The whole thing was a trap, luring us into that raid. We stole four hundred grand, shedding some blood along the way. Right after, we found out five million was missing. Looking back, it's clear Orloff stole it, leaving behind a part for us. He made it look like someone else robbed them, and set us up to take the fall. What could we do? Complain to the boss? 'Sure, we ripped you off, but only for a part of it, your wife's brother is the real crook.' Ever since, we've been running around like roaches under a kitchen light, scampering for cover. They brought in Serov and we've been dragging him around from hit to hit, trying to pin the heist on some snitches. He's not stupid. He's going to figure out we've been scamming him. Maybe he already has. Now we have to hunt down AZ, plant a few bricks of the money on him, and kill him. And then pray that's enough."

"Usher works for the mob," Shelley said. "They fed him the information, they'll finger him. But do they know you were in on the raid?"

"Me? No. But they know I hang with Usher. They know he didn't carry out the heist on his lonesome."

"Maybe if you sacrificed Usher, Mitch, and Mike, that would satisfy them."

"Sal told you about Mitch and Mike? Shit." He mulled this revelation over for a moment. "It might work, but if we do the hit, we've got to make them dead enough, fast enough so they don't talk. No hospital visits, no chance to rat us out. You'd help with that?"

Click had entered the hotbox and was standing there, behind Atch. He said, "Yeah. I think we can manage a few untimely ends. Kill Usher, Mitch, Mike, and Els. Make it look like Serov did it for when the police investigate. Then we pop the Russian. That should plug all the leaks."

"Let me think it over." Atch folded his arms across his chest. "Shel? For now, type up your resignation letter. Make it good and suicidal. Usher and the chief are waiting on it."

54

WITH THE BACK of the screen directed toward Atch and Click, Shelley opened two windows on her laptop. The first was a word processor to create her note; the other, a browser. She pretended to hunt and peck, slowly working her way through her assignment.

At the same time she ran a search on Lieutenant Jess Usher, coming across a boilerplate biography on his unit's Website. *Bingo.* It confirmed her suspicions. He'd spent the early nineties as a Marine, a posted guard at the U.S. embassy in Moscow. He spoke Russian.

He controlled Serov because he interpreted everything the snitches said. Keshawn didn't know a thing but, to Serov's ears, he confessed. It was all staged, the murder drawn out into torture to make it appear that Keshawn was reluctant to give up the names of his accomplices. Usher told Keshawn the names to write down, three more snitches. Morretti was right. Usher was pulling the strings on his very own puppet assassin. Still, Serov had to be suspicious when killing this collection of nobodies, small-time pushers, and a homeless man.

Shelley went to Google translate. She typed out a sentence in English, pressed a button and received a phonetic translation to Russian. She focused on memorizing the syllables. Her life depended on it.

She composed her resignation, I-quit-I'm-so-depressed-I-could-end-it-all note. Highlighting the document, she changed the font color to non-photo blue. Then she selected certain letters that she changed to a slightly darker shade of blue. As printed it would read as a suicide note. The moment the evidence was Xeroxed, the non-photo blue would disappear and the only remaining letters on the copy would spell out: "T H I S I S A L I E." She sent the note to the office printer.

"Done," she announced.

Atch went to the block-shaped machine to collect her printouts. He glanced over the two copies of her suicide note. He handed them over to Shelley, who scribbled her signature.

"Why two copies?" Atch asked, suspicious.

"One for you and Usher," Shelley said. "One for the captain."

"Now, how are we going to catch AZ?" Atch asked.

"The same way I found him last time," Shelley said. "Low-tech." She asked for a sheet of paper. Click retrieved a single sheet and handed it to Shelley. She picked up a pen and wrote out a note.

AZ, we need to talk. Someone is coming to kill you.
Call Detective Shelley Krieg.
Give the messenger a fifty. I will pay you back.

She added her phone number. "We'll make a couple of dozen copies of this, hand it out with twenties to junkies in and around the Shaw neighborhood. AZ's territory."

"That's over a hundred city blocks," Atch said.

"We give junkies twenty-dollar bills?" Morretti said, incredulously. "That's as good as flushing money straight down the can."

"They'll have what they need to score a fresh fix," Shelley said. "The dopers will know where to find him. He's a dealer. And any dope fiend out on a night like this has to be craving a hit."

Atch studied the scrawled note. "We have until midnight. That's as long as Usher will play along with this. If we don't have AZ on our radar by then, Usher ordered me to cut our losses and smoke him out on our own."

"Cut your losses?" Shelley said. "That means killing Mira?"

"And you."

Shelley supposed Atch's bluntness meant he was seriously considering abandoning Usher and taking her advice about some well-placed bullets. *Good*, she thought. *Divide and conquer.*

55

ATCH SAT IN the rear of the truck's cabin, the muzzle of his automatic jammed against Shelley's shoulder. She rode shotgun. Click drove.

The numbing rain had let up. The clouds descended from the sky, cloaking the streets in a frigid mist. Headlights stabbed holes in the fog. Halos bloomed from streetlamps. The chill continued unabated; the radio announced that the streets would ice over by morning, with the temperature expected to hover one degree above the October cold snap of 1917.

With a trip to the bank she collected the maximum payout her ATM allowed: 25 twenties. Shelley spread them out, staring at the fan of bills. Andrew Jackson. Owned 160 slaves. Butchered Indians who gave asylum to runaways. She remembered her old preacher railing against the love of money as the root of all evil.

Morretti drove in an expanding spiral beginning at the Bundy Playground. He dubbed their mission "Find a Fiend." It wasn't hard.

Although few junkies were out braving the weather, the search team composed of Shelley, Click, and Atch encountered plenty of abandoned buildings with peeled-back plywood. With Atch staying behind to guard Shelley, Click went inside to make contact. Some of the druggies responded with a prickly defiance, vowing they'd never snitch on AZ, who had spread goodwill by distributing higher-quality junk than any other pusher. Then, when Click told them they needed only to deliver a note, when he waved a crisp twenty before their popping eyes, they all swore they could locate exactly where AZ had set up shop. With the cash crumpled in their balled-up fists, their veins jumpy and bugging, they shambled out, swarming onto the streets, a legion of shadows hunting down a quick fix.

One offered to jump onboard their truck and guide them straight to AZ's crib. He rode standing in the pick-up's bed, leaning against the cab, greeting the world as though he were a rap star poking his head through the sunroof of his own private limousine. After ten minutes Click realized the junkie didn't have a clue and dumped him on a corner.

Within an hour Click had passed out all of the flyers and cash. Shelley suggested they load up with more funds and handbills.

"On a happy, sunny day your plan would work," Atch said. "The only junkies outside on a night like this are those too brainless to get out of the rain."

Shelley's phone rang. Caller ID blocked. Atch punched the speaker phone key and handed the cellular to Shelley.

"Hello?" Shelley said.

"This is AZ. Just calling to tell ya, go to hell and leave me alone." The line went dead.

The cabin clock read 10:10 P.M.

"Let's bluff Usher," Shelley said. "Tell him we've found AZ. Tell them to bring Mira. Lure them in."

"Pull over, Sal," Atch said. The truck slowed to a stop. Atch passed pocket change to Morretti. "Hit the pay phone and call Usher. Tell him we found AZ."

"I'm tired of playing chore boy," Click said. "Call him on your cellular."

"Pay phone," Atch said. "Usher insists. This will be the last time."

Click grumbled and got out, slamming the door behind him. He shucked his thick glove and squeezed the cold coins in his bare hand.

Once Click had picked up the phone, Atch slid a suppressor over his gun's muzzle. He said, "I had to send Click out. He has a soft spot for you. I'm going to take your advice, Shel, ambush Usher and his men. But you won't be around to see it. I don't need you anymore."

Shelley popped her seatbelt buckle and turned to look him in the eye.

"Don't try getting out. I'll have five holes in you before you pull the door handle."

"And Mira?"

"I'm guessing she's already dead. Doesn't matter, she will be soon. I hate making a mess of Click's leather upholstery ..."

Whoops arose from behind the truck. "Yo! Yo! Yo!" Someone trotted up, his gait wobbly, his arm raised over his head, waving wildly.

Atch kept his gun trained on Shelley. "Make him go away or I'll kill him, too," he demanded.

She rolled down the window.

"You! You!" he shouted as he clamped both hands on the passenger door. He had a blistered face and a ragged Afro. His threadbare jacket rattled around his thin arms. "You all said AZ would toss me a fifty! He didn't provide me nothing."

"You found AZ?" Shelley asked.

"Yeah."

"Tell me where and I'll pay you the fifty."

"1580 Marion. Only you got to come calling through the alley."

Shelley leaned down to get her wallet. As she rose, she shouted, "He's got a gun."

The junkie sprang back. Atch rammed his weapon forward, aiming out of the window. When he did, Shelley grabbed his arm. The junkie took off, racing down the sidewalk screaming, "Shit! Oh, son-of-a ... Shit!"

Shelley slammed Atch's arm down against the window. Cracking his thumb backwards, she freed him of his weapon, then turned it on him.

"Don't do it, Shel," Atch said. "I can talk Usher into delivering Mira."

"Then that's exactly what you're going to do."

Click opened the driver's side door. "You tell me to call Usher and we don't even have a meeting place." He glanced at Shelley and her automatic. "Oh."

Shelley tossed her phone to Click. "Call him back. Inform Usher I've talked my way inside of AZ's compound. Let him know it's a fortress, which it probably is. Tell him I'll lower the drawbridge and let him in when I see Mira. The address is 1580 Marion Place, around back. And Click? Pass me your gun."

He set it in the cup holder.

56

IN HIS PHONE call, Click delivered a masterful performance. He described to Usher how Shelley had located AZ and convinced him to let her inside while leaving Atch and Click out in the cold. Click took responsibility, blaming himself for allowing Shelley to slip from their grasp.

Shelley continued to treat Click as the enemy. It was safer for him that way. She ordered her companions out of the car for a quick frisk. Atch yielded an ankle pistol, a .9MM pop-gun. While holding the two at gunpoint, she shucked the bullets into the mud and tossed their guns into a curbside drain. She ordered Atch into the passenger's seat and told Click to drive. Then she climbed into the back of the pick-up cab, her legs draped along the bench seat, her head tucked down. She stabbed the nose of the automatic against the back of the pas-senger's chair hard enough to make sure Atch felt its presence.

"Why are you pointing the gun only at me?" Atch asked.

"Never kill the driver," Shelley answered.

Marion Place was a few short blocks away. The alley leading to the back had a One Way sign. Click ignored it, swinging his truck down a narrow path and around a blind corner.

It was simple enough to identify which house sold dope. Only one had a yard bordered by a spiked wrought-iron fence, secu-rity cameras directed at blind spots, and an intercom at the gate.

"I'm going in alone," Shelley said. "I'm going to use AZ as bait to exchange for Mira."

"So we're no longer your hostages?" Click asked.

"I'm not going to shoot you in cold blood and I haven't got time to take you in. You can help take down Usher or you can run for cover. He's not going to like how you let me escape. I'd get out of town if I were you."

"I doubt there's any place for me to hide as long as Serov and Usher are alive," Atch said.

Shelley slid the automatic into her coat pocket and when it didn't immediately disappear, she jammed it down, tearing through the pocket lining.

"My phone?" she said. Click handed it over. She got out of the pick-up and strode toward the gate.

"What are we going to do?" Click asked.

"Wait," Atch said. "And lie our way back into Usher's good graces."

Shelley pressed the intercom button.

"Yes?" the speaker squawked.

"I'm looking for AZ."

"Don't know of nobody who goes by that name."

"Tell AZ this is the police. Tell him he can either buzz me in for a quick pow-wow after which I promise to leave him alone, or I can return with a SWAT team and raid this place. And, if you're thinking of bailing in the between time, take a look down the alley and you'll see I've got backup."

After a moment of silence, the voice responded, "I'm AZ."

The gate clicked and unlocked. Shelley walked along a flagstone path to the back door. A pair of overhead cameras pivoted, peering down at the doorstep where she stood. Two more panned the length of the alleyway.

"Place your weapon in the transaction drawer," the intercom commanded. A different voice. "I'm talking about the one you stuffed in your jacket pocket." A metal box slid out toward her. Shelley took out her automatic and twisted off the silencer. She set the two parts in the drawer.

"Divvy your jacket and raise it up. Give me a full 360, including the tuck of your pants, then show me a flash of your ankles," the voice demanded. Shelley unzipped her coat, stretched out the interior like wings, and made a full turn. She pulled up her pant cuffs, one and then the next.

The electronic bolt gave a sharp snap and the door opened inwards. "Step inside, honeybee."

The moment she entered, a young white man shoved her against a wall and gave her a quick patdown. Satisfied she was unarmed, he set her free.

Shelley made a quick survey of her surroundings. She stood in a broad room, sparsely furnished with fold-up tables and chairs. One table had coffee and sandwiches, another had an abandoned card game. Throw pillows and army surplus blankets lay scattered on the floor. Brushes, rollers, pans, and cans rested against a half-painted wall. Attached to the back wall, a bank of security monitors.

The white kid stood off to the side. On the shy side of twenty, he clutched what looked like a toy gun but certainly wasn't.

A tall black man entered the room, pointing Shelley's pistol at her. Taylor Jackson Singer.

"Let me introduce myself," he said. "Al Zahn. Folks call me AZ."

Shelley was at a loss for words.

"And this is my associate, Marbles," AZ said, pointing to the white kid. "Marbles, Lieutenant Shelley Krieg." AZ lowered his gun, set it on the fold-up table. "You are ... persistent."

"Everything you told me was a lie?" Shelley asked, still stunned. She felt sucker-punched. She wanted to punch back.

"All lies beginning to end, but for a reason," AZ said. "Ernie Grey did me solids going way back. I got word some cops killed Ernie and then Keshawn and I heard they'd come gunning for Raffi. Now, I keep a line on the police the way a pony-man rates the horses. Keeps me in business. Story is, you're square and fair. So, when I learned you were in charge of the investigation I decided to squeeze you for info. Then, when I took a look, I thought about a plainer form of squeezing. I kept checking in, trying to meet up for some news and then as time passed, I called on account of I feared for your life."

"You asshole," Shelley said. "Your Robin Hood days are done. I can finger you."

"I can appreciate how you don't appreciate what I've done," AZ said. "But don't try messing with my operations, Shelley. I got sponsors. I got juice where it counts."

"You got the fix in with some dirty cops? We'll see who stands by you when the shit hits the fan."

"Speaking of that ..." the white kid said. "We got unfriendlies." A van pulled into the alleyway. Two cops in riot gear burst out and flanked its sides.

AZ whistled. "Lieutenant, if you know what's going down, this might be the time to clue me in."

"A gang is coming here to kill you," Shelley said. "Probably four of them. They're bringing a paid assassin. He's good at what he does."

"Some gangsters looking to blast me? Doesn't make sense. I keep tight with the locals."

"They're dirty cops. And the hit man is Russian mob."

"Damn that." AZ looked at the floor, then at his comrade. "Marbles, grab the stash and cash. We'll scram out the front."

Marbles glanced out the front window. "Too late. A flat footer with a mack nudging low from his coat flap."

"If they're hauling mac-tens, they're not planning on survivors," Shelley said.

"Give them what they want, AZ," Marbles said. "Toss our bank and stash out the second-floor window."

"They're looking for five million," Shelley said. "They won't settle for less."

AZ gasped. "Five million?"

"The cops fingered you to the mob for some money they themselves stole," Shelley explained. "They plan to break in, kill you, and plant some of the loot here."

"They want millions I don't have and don't want the drugs I do have."

"And they won't leave you around to complain," Shelley said.

"*And* you brought them to my door."

A cop in riot gear strung a chain through the bars in the grate. The other end of the chain connected to the trailer hitch of a van. A second cop held a portable battering ram at the ready.

"What kind of weapons are you carrying?" Shelley asked.

"Close to nothing," AZ said. "I've never held faith in heat. I've got a few noisemakers, that's all. That's how come I keep my defenses solid. My front and backsides will stand tall to any kayo."

"They'll blast the door if they have to," Shelley said.

"Damn that," AZ said, repeating his mantra.

Shelley looked at the security-camera monitor. Serov stood by the van, arms crossed, guns in both hands. "We do have one advantage," she said. "If they start a firefight, it will attract the real police. A quick response from law enforcement will destroy their operation. They won't be able to explain their raid. They won't be able to plant the money or kill you. And I know their gunman likes a quick in and out. He's paranoid about being seen. He'll be gone before the cavalry arrives. The moment they start making real noise, they'll need to get it over and done with in minutes. If you can hold out a few minutes, that might be enough."

"I'll ring the cop shop," AZ said. "They'll bust us, but we'll live."

"You can't do that," Shelley said.

"I can't? You're not calling the shots here, Shelley."

"They have my friend as a hostage. The only reason I came here was to negotiate her freedom."

"That's downright special," AZ said. "A regular Huxtable family moment. You bring the insane cop posse to my door to help your friend. Fuck your friend."

"AZ, I've got two strikes on me," Marbles said. "If SWAT catches me holding, I'm staring down a life jolt. For me, life is as good as death."

"Okay, it's all or nothing," AZ said. "We escape now or die trying."

"Wait!" Shelley said. "I can call someone on the force. I'll tell him to come straight over with his siren blasting. He won't arrest you and the intruders will run for cover."

"One bubbletop will scare them off?"

"They'll think more are coming."

"Maybe," AZ said.

"When they back off, I'll let you walk free and clear," Shelley said. "I promise. Just let me deal with them to get my friend safe."

A kayo, a hand-held battering ram, slammed the back door, then thumped again.

"They can hammer for an hour," AZ said. "We're locked in solid as a bank vault. If his siren doesn't chase them off, we dial up SWAT and play the lawyer game."

While the futile blows continued against the door, the curses outside grew louder than the thuds.

Shelley opened her phone and dialed. "Kent?"

"Christ, Shelley what the hell kind of mess did you stick me with? They tore apart my place, Kimmy has been crying for half an hour, my girlfriend is totally freaked. A pair of patrolmen scared them off. Then Tate came by. My answers to his questions kept getting more and more stupid. He knows something's up. Christ! He arrives, finds my house ripped to shreds, Kimmy and my girlfriend terrorized, and you know what he does? He puts me on suspension."

"Are you and Kimmy okay?"

"We are so far from okay ..."

"Are you hurt?"

"No, but ..."

"I need you."

"Fuck you, Shel! Kimmy can hear me say this, but I don't care. Fuck you!"

"Fuck you!" Kimmy echoed in the background.

"It's a matter of life and death, Kent."

"Jesus, Shel! There's this resource called *the police*. Maybe you've heard of them. They protect and serve."

"I need *you*. Life and death. I need you to find a patrol car and run your siren past 1580 Marion, it's near the corner of R in Shaw. You do that and you'll scare off some folks pinning me down."

"Pinning you down? You can't take this through dispatch?"

"I can't. They've got Mira."

"Oh, good God, Shelley. You're a goddamned sociopath. You use people. You'll probably lose me my job. But okay. Fine. I'll run by with my bubbletop and siren on, but I won't be stopping or sticking my neck out for you. And come tomorrow I'm putting in for a new partner."

The battering ram quit banging. A click let Shelley know someone was on call waiting. "I've got to go. Thanks, Kent. I mean it." She switched over to the second line.

"Open the door now or I'll shoot Yasmin," Usher said.

"Her name's Yasmira."

Shelley peered at a pair of monitors displaying the area in the back of the house. The gate was ripped free. The two cops in full gear stood near the door. One held a battering ram at a limp angle, the other a tear-gas grenade launcher. The white van sat parked in the alley, its tailpipe puffing, its side panel cracked, a sniper's rifle peeking out. The Russian was somewhere offscreen. Atch and Click stood like mannequins, their badges pinned to the front of their jackets. If the neighbors saw this, they wouldn't bother calling the police. The riot squad was already here, taking down the neighborhood drug dealer.

Shelley eyed the monitor closely. Atch held a gun, Click didn't. Click had fallen out of favor. Likely as not, they planned to kill him as part of this raid.

"I don't give a damn about AZ," Shelley said into the phone. "We'll do this. Have Morretti take Mira to the back door. I'll open up. When you release her to me, we'll leave out the front."

"AZ will let you do this?" Usher asked.

"I'm holding a gun on him as we speak," Shelley said. AZ smiled and waved his gun at her.

She tried to make the deal too sweet to refuse, playing naïve to the fact that they had staked a man out front. Usher would have no reason to believe they could escape. The line went dead. Shelley hoped that meant they agreed.

"So we get your friend in here, then what do we do?" AZ asked.

"They won't come barreling in. They think I have a gun. You said this door can hold out for an hour. In ten to fifteen minutes my partner will arrive to chase them off with a siren."

On the security monitor they could see Usher guiding Mira out of the back of the van. She wore Plasticuffs on her ankles and wrists. Usher spoke into a walkie-talkie. The two in riot suits put silencers on their guns, aimed the muzzles at the lenses, and shot out the cameras.

AZ said, "After you get your girl, slam the door. The locks will drop automatically. I'm not waiting behind to see. We keep our stash in a room at the top of the stairs. Anyone charging up the steps will make for easy pickings. We'll hole up there."

"It's going to work out," Shelley said. "Trust me."

57

A SERIES OF heavy thumps rattled the back door.

"It's Morretti. I've got your girlfriend."

Without the security cameras' feed, Shelley felt utterly blind.

"I want to hear her," Shelley said.

"Her mouth is kind of bundled up in mummy's tape. They didn't like her attitude. She's standing next to me, you've got my word."

Shelley slid the drawer out. "Drop your gun into the transaction drawer."

"The only gun I've got is pressed against my back."

Shelley thought, *The moment I open the door they'll shoot all three of us.*

Outside the door a muttered argument began. Shelley pressed an ear against the frigid metal. She couldn't pick up words but recognized Usher's and Click's voices. Shelley tried picturing how many more were out there waiting. The two in riot gear. The one with the sniper's rifle. They would station two out front to cut down anyone trying to escape. Serov was nearby. Atch was a wild card.

"I'm going to open the door," Shelley said. "Mira, spring straight inside and drop to the floor. If anyone else tries entering, I'll shoot them." She had no gun.

She ran over in her mind what she had to do. *Open the door, grab Mira, yank her inside. Click, too. Slam the door before gunfire takes all of us down. I only need to be faster than a speeding bullet.*

Shelley clasped the doorknob. It felt ice-cold. A single throw switch controlled both of the door's bulky electronic locks. A sharp clack announced the bolts' release. *Thwap!*

The door swung inwards. Mira stood there, her lower face masked with gauze, her arms drawn behind her, her feet tied. Behind her stood Click, behind him Usher. Click shot a swift kick backwards against Usher's knee. Usher, his gun drawn and aimed at the entryway, swiveled in pain as he squeezed the trigger. The hollow-point blasted a crater in the brick wall.

Click thrust Mira forward, and together they stumbled over the threshold, falling to the floor as more gunfire from the two men in riot gear pocked the metal door. A bullet snagged Click's leg as he collapsed on top of Mira, pinning her to the floor. As Shelley stiff-armed the door to shut it, Usher unleashed a spring coil baton, a steel rod that, with a flick of his wrist, extended to thirty-two inches, its tip lodging in the doorway. Instead of sealing shut, the door bounced back. A hail of bullets skidded off the door's metal plating, lodging in the plaster wall.

This time Shelley threw her full weight against the door while shouting at Click and Mira, "Get upstairs." The baton still prevented the door from closing as bullets thudded its exterior. Click grabbed his wounded leg and struggled to his feet. He slung one arm around Mira, and together they began clumping and staggering up the stairs.

Shelley kept her back pressed to the door, her feet firmly planted. The police outside gave the door another whack with their battering ram, slamming it with the impact of a cannonball. Shelley tumbled forward, then scrambled to her feet. A tear-gas canister landed near her and ignited, its caustic liquid rapidly turning into a mist. Shelley held her breath and grabbed its scalding shell, searing her hand as she chucked it back out the door. The two police in riot gear and gas masks stormed in through the fumes. Shelley grabbed a portable table by its leg, flipped it over, and hurled it at their feet. As they dodged to the side, she leaped into the hallway and plunged hands first onto the steps. She scrambled furiously on all fours up the stairs, then flattened herself against the landing floor as bullets sailed over her.

AZ fired down from above, erratic blasts to notify the intruders that the occupants were armed and ready to fight back. The invading force halted fire, staking out their positions. In the moments of relative silence, Shelley clambered up the remaining steps.

AZ let her into the upstairs bunker but didn't close the door. "This door is aluminum," he said. "It won't stop a battering ram." He kept his gun aimed down the stairwell. Above the landing, a convex mirror allowed him to see the bottom of the stairs. "Our only chance is to stop them from coming up."

"And thanks for letting them in," Marbles said. He looked behind the curtain through the bars that guarded the window, studying the street out front.

"They don't seem to give a fuck about making noise," AZ said.

Click sat on the floor, blood percolating from his leg. He cut Mira's hands free with his penknife. Mira pulled the swath of gauze down far enough to take a deep breath. Then she unfastened her belt, cinching it around Click's thigh.

Shelley looked around the mostly barren room. A police scanner sat atop pumice blocks. A dresser had its drawers half-opened. The bottom drawer was stuffed with rolls of paper money. Inside the top drawer were neatly stacked rows of filled and capped hypodermic needles. A pot-bellied hand grenade rested atop a metal trunk near an ashtray with two half-burnt joints.

"How long did you say we got to hold out before a SWAT team gets here?" Marbles asked. "Ten minutes?"

The police scanner squawked. "This is 237. We're hearing gunfire northwest sector near the corner of Marion and R."

"Hold off," the dispatcher said. "A special-forces operation is underway."

"Shit," Click said, grimacing, pinching his leg. "Let me call this in. I'll tell them there's an officer down. Me."

AZ tossed him his phone.

"One sentry out front," Marbles said. "Not packing obvious heat. Talking into a two-way like he's running the show."

"How much ammo you got, Marbles?" AZ asked.

Marbles sprang his fingers up twice, totaling two tens.

"Damn that," AZ said. He raised four fingers.

"The grenade?" Shelley asked.

"It's a cigarette lighter," AZ said.

Mira cut the Plasticuffs from her ankles. She raised the pen-knife. "If they attack, I've got a sword."

Shelley peered down the stairwell.

"Why are they so quiet?" Mira asked.

"Preparing their attack," Shelley said.

"Okay, then. What's our plan?"

"Staying alive," AZ said.

Mira nodded. "Good plan."

Shelley inspected the drawer full of hypodermics. "You sell junk already prepared in needles?"

"Keeps back the bug," AZ said. "Only it's not junk. It's my own blend, a double-whammy of Alfenta and LAAM. Alfenta gives the same high as junk but it holds steady when ready-mixed. LAAM lasts as long as methadone. Put together, the dopers get the buzz of shooting smack but not the fall-off. A junkie can live a day without. The fiends are grinning, the looting is down, and my fanboys on the force give me the wink. They let me sling my trade."

"You're a regular saint," Shelley said.

"Public angel number one. You may not be able to wrap your mind around this, but I do this as a community service. As long as junkies come to me, they don't get the bug, they don't overdose, and they can live a day on a jolt. They keep steady and healthy and the neighborhood thrives."

Click slapped the phone closed. "The boys downstairs tried hanging a do-not-disturb sign on this operation. I convinced dispatch it's gone belly up and we need backup and a med team. Five minutes. Tops."

The scanner announced, "Available units, Northwest sector, 1580 Marion, officer injured, operation underway."

"We've got backup on the way," Shelley shouted down the stairs.

"Then we'll have to make this fast," Usher called back.

"Atch!" Shelley yelled. "I don't suppose you're considering what we discussed?"

Atch said to Usher, "The bitch tried to talk us into killing you."

Usher fired a bullet point-blank into Atch's skull.

"No, he's not considering it," Usher called up. "Atch was a fuck-up. And, Morretti? You've chosen who you want to die with. Fuck you and fuck your partner."

Usher spoke over his shoulder, shouting some words in Russian.

Shelley knew Serov stood within hearing range. She realized this might be her only chance. She spoke the Russian phonetic syllables she had memorized. "Josef, Usher lgal vam. Eti lyudi, kotorykh ty ubival ne vory. Vy videli ikh, vy eto znayete. Usher ukral den'gi." *Josef. Usher has lied to you. These people you've been killing are not the thieves. You have seen them, you know this. Usher stole the money.*

An argument began in Russian between Josef and Usher, the tone at first strained and then quickly intensifying. It ended with Usher unleashing a barrage of shouting that trailed off into pleading. The only intelligible words were: Orloff! Orloff! Orloff!

Gunfire erupted, not just between Usher and Serov, but from several sources at once. After a half minute the volleys stopped and for a moment all was quiet.

Usher stumbled up the stairs, falling to all fours, trying to escape Serov, who strode behind him. Already bleeding, Usher collapsed on the landing. Serov ended the lieutenant's struggle with a headshot. Usher twitched, then moved no more.

Marbles unloaded a clip, firing blindly, keeping his body behind the metal door. Serov disappeared down the steps.

"Bullet count?" AZ asked.

"Ten down," Marbles said. "Ten to go."

They could see Serov standing motionless at the bottom of the stairs, his image reflected in the curved mirror. He glared back at them. His trench coat stood parted. A pair of leather bands criss-crossed his shirt. Each held a dozen magazines. He held .22 automatics in both hands.

"This is the Russian assassin," Shelley said. "He's good at what he does. He killed the others. If he draws to shoot you, he won't miss."

Marbles and AZ waved their guns so he could see them. Shelley approached the top of the stairs with the hand grenade butane lighter, one finger threatening to pull its pin. In the distance, a siren wailed.

Then Shelley raised her telephone and took a snapshot, this one a distorted image of the assassin reflected in the convex mirror.

The guns, the phony hand grenade, and the siren were not enough to get a reaction out of Serov. The photo did. Serov raised an automatic and trailed its barrel down the light switch. His reflection disappeared.

58

THE FIRST FLOOR remained dark as Shelley, Mira, Click, AZ, and Marbles waited. The police siren drew nearer and nearer.

Shelley looked out of the front window. Kent's car rolled down the street toward them and then passed, a portable siren flashing on its roof. "AZ, Marbles, grab what you can and run."

"And the Russian?" AZ asked.

"He's gone. He picks his fights and then disappears."

The two dealers stuffed a duffel bag full of money, leaving behind hundreds of hypodermics.

Mira and Shelley offered their hands to Click, helping him to his feet. Together, they clumped down the stairs, stepping over Lieutenant Usher's corpse on the landing. On the first floor, Shelley flipped on the light switch.

The carnage was grisly. Efficient at the headshot, Serov had left behind bodies with pools of blood spreading out from ripped-open skulls. Two Prince George's cops lay on the floor in their riot gear. One had no visible wounds, but blood filled the goggles of his gas mask. The other had a razor wire twisted around his neck along with a headshot. Atch had a bullet in his temple.

A DC patrolman had swung open a refrigerator door to use as cover. Five bullets had pierced the door in a vertical line, the topmost also piercing his forehead. He sat back to the wall, his body limp, a discarded marionette. His name tag read Ellesmore. Els. Alongside him sat several blocks of hundred-dollar bills wrapped in butcher paper. *Benjamin Franklin*, Shelley noted. *Quaker*.

"Shel, let me take it from here," Click said. "I'll get my truck and drive myself to the hospital. I'd rather bullshit my way through a gunshot wound than try to explain this slaughterhouse."

In the distance, a chorus of overlapping sirens.

Shelley squeezed Mira's hand. "Time to face the music."

Now that the gunfire had died down, the neighborhood was lit up, residents venturing to their windows.

As Shelley and Mira stepped down from the porch, Kent's car pulled up, driving in reverse. He rolled down his window. "Are you okay?" he asked.

Shelley peered at the back seat, looking for Kimmy. Empty. "I'm okay," she said.

"I'll live," Mira added.

"You saved our asses, Kent," Shelley said. "Take Mira home before the police arrive. I'll be at the station. I'll probably be there for the next few hours. Or the next few years. I've got some explaining to do."

AZ and Marbles trotted down from the porch, then skidded to a halt upon seeing the car's flashing siren. Shelley said, "Kent, this is Alfred Zahn and a friend."

"Jesus, Shel, you collared AZ?"

"Not quite," Shelley said. "They got away. Take them wherever they want to go."

"Thanks," AZ said, flinging his duffel bag into the back of Kent's car. It spilled out wads of bills.

"Jesus, Shel," Kent repeated.

Two patrol cars approached from the end of the street.

"Thanks, Kent," Shelley said. "And for the good of your career, none of this happened." She thumped the roof of Kent's car with a farewell pat.

Kent drove off.

Shelley raised her detective's badge over her head to greet the arriving officers.

59

"Detective Krieg," Shelley announced as the officers exited their cars. "Multiple homicides. We have officers fallen inside. No one living. We need to secure the scene. Divide yourselves front and in the alley."

As the next group arrived, she said, "Detective Krieg. We have fallen officers in the house. Respect the perimeter. Wait here for senior command."

An ambulance joined the police cars that had transformed Marion Place into a parking lot. Shelley watched as a car screeched to a stop and Captain Tate got out.

He looked her over, his eyes hard as quartz. "Detective Krieg."

"Captain. Five bodies, all officers, including Atchison, another Metro, and three with PG."

"And how did you come to be here?"

"I was heading to Kent's apartment. Someone had broken in. Along the way I overheard the call and responded here, first on scene."

"You need to come up with better lies or learn to take the Fifth," Tate said. "I'll take over from here on. I recommend you fly on home and work on your story. We'll meet first thing tomorrow. Consider yourself suspended pending a full inquiry."

"Yes, sir."

"And Detective Krieg. I know Atchison was corrupt. I know you're a good officer. Don't worry. I can make this go away."

Shelley squinched her eyes in disbelief. His pronouncement seemed impossible, unreal. "Thank you, sir."

As Tate began issuing orders, Shelley stood motionless for a few moments, uncertain what to do next. She couldn't call a cab and she couldn't be seen walking down this street, in effect announcing she hadn't brought her car. She decided to walk through the murder house and leave via the back alley.

While passing one of the corpses in riot gear, she noticed a set of car keys dangling from his jacket pocket. It displayed a circle with three shields: a Buick. She pocketed the keys and exited out the back door.

In the alleyway, she saluted the officer securing the scene. Then she pressed the Buick's key, listening for a tweet. Not hearing one, she followed the alley up to R Street. From here, the car answered her summons with a blink and chirp.

She opened its door. They'd left the interior light on, the glove compartment open: obviously in a hurry to be killed.

She slid into the driver's seat and pushed the seat back. Adjusting the mirror, she studied her face. For the first time in days, she felt at peace.

As she prepared to crank the engine, she imagined for a moment: This time the car will explode. Mob roulette. *Of course not. They wouldn't rig their own car to explode.* The engine started without drama or surprise.

It neared two A.M. when she drove up the alleyway behind her house. She wasn't heading home. She reached into her jacket pocket and pressed the button on the remote for Ruth Ann's garage. She got out and placed Cassidy into the Buick's back seat. She removed him from the body bag, maggots and all.

DRIVING PAST THE Evarts Street AME, she saw a patrol car parked outside. So many hours later, they were still working the homicide in the church. In the back of the vehicle sat the old lady and feral child. *Witnesses? Or merely being transported to social services?*

Shelley drove two more blocks, a distance close enough to be connected to the other crime, but far enough not to be noticed immediately. She swabbed clean where she imagined her fingerprints might be. Then she got out, abandoning the car.

She walked in the bitter cold, taking the back streets, headed to Mira's place.

She would camp out there for a couple of days, away from the crosshairs of the investigation. She imagined how it would play out, a sequence of events as unstoppable as an avalanche. Her 911 call from the church would lead investigators to her house with its busted-in, bullet-ridden garage door hiding a junked car and a bullet-blasted lock on the entrance to the house. Either that, or a passing neighbor would see the damage and call the police.

But hadn't Tate promised to make all of this go away?

She took out her cellular and cupped it in her hand, staring at it as she walked, wanting to call Taylor Jackson Singer. AZ.

No. This is not me. He's a criminal, a drug-slinger. This is some byproduct of the dangers we shared, adrenaline as Krazy Glue, with the emphasis on Krazy.

She scrolled through her recent calls. His number appeared on her phone's screen. She pressed SEND. Three rings and then his voice mail kicked in. She hung up.

60

Lt. Salvatore Morretti, wearing a cast on his left leg, limped in to the Third District Station on Monday afternoon. Summoned by Captain Tate, he had been instructed to appear "dead or alive."

Sal explained to his fellow officers that he had shot himself in the leg while practicing his quick draw. "Click! Click!" the officers jibed.

Tate ordered Shelley and Click into his office, where he demanded a full confession. When they finished recounting all the details, their experiences and suspicions, he granted them absolution. "I've lost one detective over this," he declared. "I'm not losing two more. I'll write the official story. You'll memorize it."

The official story: The Russian mob had tried to muscle in on DC territory. The photos of Serov in the church and in AZ's dope house proved their involvement. In particular, the second photo placed the hit man at the scene of the slaughter. When the police investigated the Buick with Cassidy's body, they ran the vehicle ID number. It belonged to a Vadim Orloff, the brother-in-law of a Maryland mob boss. The next day, the police raided his house, where they discovered him lying dead on his kitchen floor, his ribs cracked open, all of his fingers lopped off except for his thumb.

Lieutenant Jess Usher, head of the Narcotics Division of the Major Crimes Unit in Prince George's and an expert on the local presence of the Russian mob, had coordinated—with the help of DC Metro—a late-night strike at what was believed to be a low-level, non-aggressive target. With Captain Tate's approval, Metro Detective Kris Atchison and Patrolman Reese Ellesmore joined in the raid. Once there, they encountered unforeseen resistance that included a known mob enforcer, Josef Serov. All the officers were killed. Their murderers fled the scene, abandoning a cache of drugs and several bricks of bills, totaling forty thousand dollars.

On that Sunday night at the time of the raid, Detective Krieg had been working on a murder case with Serov as the suspect. While passing through the Shaw neighborhood, she responded to the initial call for help and was first on scene. The roles played by Click, Mira, AZ, and Marbles were left out of the report.

Tate relieved Shelley and Kent of their suspensions. "They never happened," he said.

DC Metro released Rafael Hooks from custody, dropping all charges and issuing an official apology to him and his family for his arrest for a murder now proven to be part of a mob squabble. His lawsuit continued.

By Friday, the investigation into the affair languished, the conclusion pending the capture of Serov and his associates. Tate demanded that all new lines of inquiries be routed through him.

"FIVE OFFICERS DEAD, two jurisdictions, and everyone is playing 'Don't ask, don't tell?'" Agent Ballinger twisted his angel hair pasta around his fork. He sat across from Shelley. The day was warmer than November should be and the bistro had extended its seating onto the sidewalk.

"Nobody wants to smear the dead," Shelley said. "Besides, they've got Serov and Orloff to act as the bogeymen."

"Thanks for those photos. They gave me a boost with my standing at the Bureau. Finally, I'm chasing someone with a face." He'd asked for his Alfredo sauce as a side dish. He dunked a forkful of noodles in it. "By the way, who took that second photo?"

"It was found on Lt. Atchison's phone."

"But how did it get on his phone? My expert tells me the aspect ratio doesn't match his phone's camera. Furthermore, his phone card has no record of receiving it. My guy also told me, judging from the angle, that it was taken from the top of the stairs at a height of six-foot-two."

"Really? I'm six-foot-four."

"You held the camera at eye level."

"Or else it was a five-foot blonde holding a camera over her head."

"So how did you get that shot of Serov still hanging around the crack house when you didn't arrive until after the killings?"

"It was a smack house. There's a difference."

"And?"

"And no further comment. By the way, you didn't seem surprised to discover I'm not a five-foot blonde."

"I called ahead," Ballinger said. "Did my research. Do you have a guy?"

"Are you still hitting on me?"

"Still trying. You've got a vibe. You're what I call a tall drink of ..."

"Don't finish that sentence," Shelley warned. "If you ever want to date a tall woman, never say that."

"Hmm."

"Besides, I've got someone."

On Friday, at the end of her shift, Shelley turned over to Captain Tate the final draft of her confidential report.

He thanked her for it, adding, "Consider it buried."

As he set the folder in his desk drawer, Shelley noticed a smudge of ink, non-photo blue, near the tip of his index finger and thumb. She stood there a moment, frozen.

"This isn't the military," Tate said. "You don't have to wait to be dismissed."

She muttered, "Right," opened the door, and turned to leave.

"Relax this weekend," he said, not unkindly, as she departed. "You've earned it."

While driving home, Shelley thought about the ink stain. What did it mean? She supposed more than a few people used those markers. Still, Atch had mentioned someone called "chief," one of the gang who had never been identified. What had Marbles said? He saw a person standing near the front of the house, talking on a two-way, looking like the boss. And how did Tate manage to show up at the crime scene so soon? How had he happened to show up at Bellotti's apartment? And who else but someone with clout and access could have made documents and case files disappear from the archives?

But then why did Tate take Atch and Click off the case? Perhaps he thought it would be a slam dunk and didn't want his man Atch to be part of the investigation that would kick in after Raffi's murder. *He knew they were going to kill Raffi. He chose me because he wanted to paint a black face on the fiasco.* Later, when things went sour, he put Atch back in charge.

But the real proof came from how far Tate had bent over backwards to implement the cover-up. By wiping out the trail, he was protecting himself.

Whom should she tell? Kent? Sal? If Tate suspected they knew, their lives would be in danger.

IAD? Ballinger? What evidence did she have? Even the photos with the marker on Keshawn's fingers had disappeared. Atch had weeded documents from the official file and shredded the duplicates. The negatives must exist some-where. Or else not. The cover-up had been cold-blooded and thorough in all other matters.

Even worse, probing into the matter would unravel the official story. She, Sal, and Kent would be fired–and maybe prosecuted–for making false statements.

SHE SUMMED UP the situation to Mira over breakfast. "All I have to go on is blue fingers."

"Does he still have that suicide note you wrote?"

"He said he tore it up."

"I don't suppose you dated it?"

Shelley shook her head.

"Doing nothing makes sense to me," Mira said. "Tate's not the only one who covered this up. You did, too. And, if every-thing got out, I'd probably lose my job as well."

Shelley picked at her grapefruit slice with a serrated spoon. "I can't get him out of my mind," she said.

"Who?"

"Taylor."

"Zahn?"

"AZ."

"The drug dealer."

"Robin Hood," Shelley said. "I looked up the drugs. It's like he's running a freelance methadone clinic. What's so wrong with that?"

"You being a cop, I can think of several things." Mira shook her head. "You're a strong, intelligent woman, Shel. You'd be throwing your career away for some Disney dream."

"Disney?"

"I seem to recall Disney making a Robin Hood movie. They filled it with adorable dancing foxes. And I seem to recall Maid Marian got thrown in a dungeon."

"I must be crazy. I don't even know how to find him."

Mira shrugged. "You're a detective. Hunt him down."

"Now you're saying I should go for it?"

"I was thinking for you it's a step up. Letting go. Getting stupid for love."

"So you like being the more sensible one."

Mira smiled. "Oh yeah."

Acknowledgments

When I first imagined setting my story in DC, I knew it had to be set in the vibrant urban life of the city and not in the political machine that makes up the nation's capital. In my years in Washington, my occasional interactions with national politics left me feeling they were as alien as another planet. I knew this novel had to be set in the city I came to know and love through bus rides, through bicycling, through long walks, through Howard University's radio station, and through its neighborhoods. So I thank DC for all of its jazz and brassiness.

I thank the bloggers and others who shared life stories that provided me with insight into the joys and challenges of growing up a tall child and becoming a tall woman.

I thank David Simon for creating the Rosetta Stone of police procedurals, the non-fiction book *Homicide: A Year on the Killing Streets* and all of his work to define the modern urban rhythms of crime and punishment.

I thank John Dufresne for his guidance in writing.

I thank Bob Ritchie and my mother, Adelina Ortiz de Hill, for reading and reviewing early drafts of this manuscript.

Finally, special thanks to Christian Alighieri of Ransom Note Press for guidance, critiques, editing, and intensive feedback.